GW01034072

Originally published under the title *Pontescuro*
by Miraggi Editioni, in Turin, Italy in 2019.

Published in the United States in 2024
by August Crime, an imprint of

Clevo Books
530 Euclid Ave #45
Cleveland, Oh 44115
www.clevobooks.com

Library of Congress Control Number: 2024932477

ISBN: 9781685770051
E-book ISBN: 9781685770068

Printed in the USA

Exterior and interior design: Ron Kretsch

First American Edition

Pontescuro

by Luca Ragagnin

Illustrated by Enrico Remmert

Translation by Mary Jean Lutz Bujdos and Jamie Richards

Preface to the English Edition

When it appeared in 2019, the dense, sophisticated yet gripping novel that you are about to read was nominated for the Premio Strega, Italy's most prestigious narrative prize. The nomination was certainly a function of its striking style and technique, which are the result of the author's long and varied writing career. Luca Ragagnin, born in 1965 in Turin, has written songs, plays, essays, and poems, coming to the novel form only in the last decade. *Pontescuro* clearly benefits from such a rich narrative experience. Not only is the plot narrated from the multiple perspectives of human and non-human witnesses to the crime that constitutes its dark center, but the novel conveys the tragic and lyrical qualities of the landscape and the characters thanks to a poetic language full of expressive force. The voices of its human and non-human narrators are rendered with theatrical emotion, and they immerse the reader in a credible yet slightly fantastic intrigue.

A tragic sensibility was indeed needed for this narration, as darkness and evil pervade the novel, as intimated in the title, "ponte scuro", which in Italian means "dark bridge". As we progress through the short chapters, each narrated by a different voice, we soon understand that evil is present also in the little village of the same name which surrounds the bridge.

On the one hand, we have the archaic, feudal environment that in 1922 was still typical of the Italian Northern countryside: living in a castle on the only hill of the region, we have the stark, unflinching landowner, with his three sons and a daughter, Dafne. This setting is both realistic and imaginative, and the narration and its atmosphere are closer to the fairy tale than to the historical novel. Still, the evocation of the Fascist March on Rome – which did originate in the Italian agrarian North – is vivid and effective. Two of the brothers are directly involved in the March: the oldest as a supporter, the second as a fallen opponent. The third brother is much more discreet but far more important: he does not claim to take a position either in the historical or the personal events narrated in the book, but remains not only as a witness, but also the illustrator of the story, penciling the delicate drawings that accompany the narration.

Like the youngest brother, the reader is a witness to a double crime: one is perpetrated at the social and political level, with the oppressive land-owning hierarchies falling in line with Fascism among widespread fear and ignorance; the second one is a function of the sexist and hypocritical morality of provincial Italy, where women's agency is stifled but their sexuality a very public affair. The protagonists of the intrigue are Dafne, the rebellious and sexually threatening daughter of the local lord, and Ciaccio, a foundling who mysteriously appears as a newborn and becomes her friend. We soon realize that these two are the only innocents in the story, and they will both suffer for that. Surrounded and understood only by the forces of the landscape – the birds, the insects, the bridge, the omnipresent fog – they can only express their sensitive natures by shocking or escaping the village's stifling atmosphere. They meet in the fields, near the river, and they trust each other because they recognize their shared difference.

The protagonists do have a fairy tale quality about them: we have the beautiful princess prisoner in her unfeeling father's castle, and the village idiot who is unjustly persecuted but finally succeeds in escaping his cruel surroundings. The fact that the story sounds credible and historically appropriate is perhaps Ragagnin's greatest accomplishment. In this little masterpiece, we also hear the echo of other powerful evocations of Italian society in the first years of Fascism. Here I will only mention Alberto Moravia's *Il Conformista* (*The Conformist*) and Carlo Emilio Gadda's *Quer Pasticciaccio Brutto di Via Merulana* (*That Awful Mess in Via Merulana*). The reader will also remember *Novecento* (*1900*), the cinematic masterpiece by Bernardo Bertolucci, that also situates its sexual-political plot in the Po Valley. These true Italian modern classics might be the next step for the English-speaking readers of *Pontescuro*, who will certainly come out of their experience fascinated and asking for more. The implicit relation between male arrogance and the fear of women's sexuality on the one hand, and the appeal of authoritarian social and political practices on the other are present in all these works, which are realized in a poetic, tragic style that steers clear of all the pedantic pitfalls of realism. It goes to the credit of the English translators to have been able to render such a spellbinding narrative style thanks to her fidelity to the Italian original.

Neither Ragagnin nor his predecessors have easy answers to the ultimate reasons of the evil circulating in Italian society in the 1920s and 30s, nor to its obdurate persistence throughout history. But it is through narratives like these that we get closer to a reality that is too important to remain unspoken.

—*Giuseppina Mecchia, University of Pittsburgh*

The times we lived in were truly a tale told by an idiot
Full of sound and cruelty

Zbigniew Herbert (Trans. Alissa Valles)

one

[closed names]

They were called Giovanni, Tonio, Puccio, Giorgione. They were called Luigi, Mario, and Bandiera, the last of whom thought he'd been given a girl's name and wanted revenge. They were called Guglielmetto, Rico, Luciano. And there was the fat, voluptuous, unhappy Nella. She was convinced that she knew about love, but it wasn't true. They were called Michelino, Franchino, Enrico. There was Paolo di Ca' Bassa and Paolo di Ca' Alta, and of course they couldn't stand each other. Then there was a guy who lived even further up named Cosimo who had three sons and a daughter. The daughter's name was Dafne, which means laurel. They were called Gené, who didn't have a thought in his head, and Emilio, a.k.a. Zuntura, the handyman, who could fix everything but his own heart. They were called Làinfondo, "over there"; because he'd never been given a name so he was called by the general direction in which he lived. They were called Ciaccio, like a bird's caw; Don Andreino and Don Antonio, because they were the priests; and there was Furàza, clam, something you can't open without killing. There was the town and others who lived in town, not many—a few kids, a couple of old ladies, animals. The town was called Pontescuro: once upon a time, there was Pontescuro. And everyone there, from oldest to youngest, even those without a nickname, were like Furàza. They had many names, but they were all closed, for if they were opened they would die. They were called blind sky, weary and heavy earth, their names were cursed bridges and wrecked boats. They were called bare branches, pebbles, straw, dried mud, manure, winter chill, and summer swelter. They were called Eugenio Romanelli, a stranger who didn't know the rules of Pontescuro. A man, who arrived there one day, observed everything, and cracked the town open. It was 1922. A long, long time ago. The fog was there to hide everything.

two

[merciful fog]

You know fog? They say it's bad for people. One of those sayings that start going around one day, no one knows how, and then that day is lost in time. Or rather, in the night of time—the fog of time. And so the origins of this serious, authoritative statement that fog is bad disappear, likewise, in time. The allegation remains, looming over the generations to come. The children become adolescents, then adults, then old people, then nothing more; they leave this world, taking their belief in that allegation along with them. This is no tall tale, you know. The fog has always been an important presence around these parts, one of those intangible things that, just by seeing it from this point or that, or being inside it, determines who you are, because it carries your name, decides the kind of house you sleep in, and on what bed, and if it is a bed at all. There is nothing magical about it, don't worry, it's simply the lay of this land, its scattered houses like single or crowded or hidden teeth in the mouth of the plain. But before I tell you any more about Pontescuro—that's the name of this town, and so the name of the mouth that mashed up this story—I want to tell you a little about me. Maybe the first person to blurt out a statement like "fog is bad for people," meant something else entirely. Maybe he was just joking around. Maybe he was on his way home with a friend after convincing the barkeep to stay open late, and leaving town, the crowded teeth, and stumbling toward their hovels, two single teeth, and I was there too, only for a bit, as I sleep at night of course, and the one slurred to the other that it wasn't cheap wine that brought on thoughts of death, it was the fog. Or maybe the accusatory expression came from a grandmother, exasperated by her little granddaughter who instead of sleeping kept kicking off the covers and scrambling over to the window, looking out into the town's early darkness, for something all her own, a detail, something magical, a branch or nocturnal creature, or a light further off—but the grandmother must have thought it was the fog that captivated the child; the fog that slipped away as fast as the covers on her bed.

I feel a little sorry for all the men and women who, even as adults, remain stuck in childhood.

People go looking for all kinds of reasons to feel bad, and think that's taking care of themselves: life for me, death for you. They don't realize that every breath we take brings us closer to death.

They say that the fog gets into your lungs and destroys them, that the fog warps the cars, that the fog makes you forget all the thoughts you need to keep going and replaces them with others that make you lose your way completely.

Never mind that, in 1922, few motor cars were on the road, and moreover, in Pontescuro, death had been long away, and wasn't looking for me, I assure you.

But now I'd better make myself scarce. There's a whole town of poor, oblivious wretched waiting to take shape.

three

[the bridge between two nothings]

Pontescuro, were it up to me, would indicate another village, another story, other people. Instead, it means me. Of course, it's because of the bridge there in the middle of all the houses. In fact, the bridge came first, and then the houses. Odd, no? There used to be nothing here except that, insisting on its raison d'être: the river below.

In the days of that early settlement, the Po River flowed undisturbed, protected by the fog. On the edge of one bank: nothing. On the edge of the other: nothing.

I'm talking about a very long time ago, obviously.

First the bridge was built, and then all the rest, on both one side and the other. It was murky, that stone bridge, because no one understood what it was for.

"Why connect two nothings?" the women asked the builders.

"Because if we only build houses on one bank, no one will ever want to go to the other," they replied.

That reasoning was a little hard to follow, but in the end, it was airtight—or rather, watertight.

And so, the town developed in a circle around a short straight line. And that's how you should imagine me now: a circle, divided horizontally or vertically depending on your perspective, like the partition of a secret or a still-fresh animal carcass.

The continuity of this place is in its interruption.

That's how I am, but I'm not the only one. The people who were born and raised here are made out of interruption. And of everyday secrets watered down by the elements of this land.

See, it might seem like a paradox, but if everyone knows everything about everyone in these little rural communities still today, let alone in the twenties, this same condition also makes it possible to protect a secret or unconfessable sin in the best possible hiding place—before the villagers' eyes, right in their faces, like a sudden chill.

four

[not everything can be controlled]

But let's say you are about to enter Pontescuro, on the only road that leads there from the big city.

We won't ask who you are or why you're here. We'll find out sooner or later, on our own. For the moment, we want to welcome you, as any visitor deserves.

"We don't have an inn here, Mister, but if you'd like to stay overnight, we will find you suitable accommodations.

"You see, there's a hundred of us, roughly counted: fifty souls here on the south side, and as many over on the other. Our houses are made out of stone and straw, and fortunately, no one from the capital has ever ordered us to change things. To renovate and rehabilitate, as they would say down there. And thank goodness. We're attached to our straw and stone. They've taken root in our hearts, and are our friends.

"What's that you say? Ah, yes, that up there. It's true, it's impossible to miss. Kind of because it's on the only big hill we have, but mostly because it's a place you wish you could stay in.

Cavernous rooms warmed by countless fireplaces, fresh, fragrant linens, generous libations and hospitality. That's how you picture it, right? Us too, except the hospitality. We've never been inside it. And never will.

"That castle belongs to Signor Casadio, and we can assure you that he will never host you or anyone else. We rarely even see him in town. Even though we all work for him.

"All the land you can see, as far as the horizon, is his property.

"And the boats that pass so slowly under the dark bridge, those are his too.

"He's the owner of everything, but not everything can be controlled. Tomorrow morning, when you're already on your way, you'll realize it."

five

[the rugged boats]

"We have tree branches for veins, sawdust for blood. We're slow and rugged and chug along until we die. Fish steer clear of us, and only one man guides us, up there in front. He has never smiled, not even once. But to and fro, to and fro, he leads us.

"And we're promises for others, too. We venture far from Pontescuro. But we can smell our surroundings and sail just under that bridge, a roof over the heads of all the drowned.

"We are Casadio's boats. We are the arks of sacred commerce.

"And you stay here not because you are the exploited.

"We know, as we set off, that is what you believe.

"You stay here because you're guilty.

"All of you except one: the one who will pay."

six

[Cosimo Casadio and his ledgers]

"With such scarce austerity among humanity's lower ranks, people unworthy even of suffering, I hole up in my castle. You people have no idea, all you do is point fingers. I'd like to see you in my place, I'd love to be in one of your hovels spying on you, if you were Cosimo Casadio, a landowner from birth, the master of this castle from birth, in 1852.

"On the side of wrong by birthright, you would say, if you'd been able to study books instead of just hay and fire.

"If a person is seen as wrong from birth, how should they act, what should they do? Wait until they grow up and then throw it all into the bushes? Or exploit the power of land and money and no longer look anyone in the eye? Become even more cruel? I didn't do that, even if no one believes it.

"I didn't do that. You haven't the slightest idea what full-fledged power really is. You don't even know where to find it. My boats, the boats that you lead into murkier waters, into the big city, they know how power works over there. I've done nothing but seek fairness, but it's just not possible with so many heads beneath you.

"I keep my ledgers in the parlor, and I update them every evening, by the chill of an extinguished fire. The columns for give and take, deadlines, new loads, new deliveries, new cargo, which tomorrow, turning the page, will become old loads and deliveries and cargo, and it's up to me to go on, and update it again. That's it. This is my inhumanity. No more to it than that.

"There used to be children, and a wife who left us far too soon.

"What do you expect?"

seven

[the first son marches]

"I am Giacomo Casadio, the firstborn. I'm thirty-four, and I'm not here.

"I am one of the thirty thousand little black dots marching on Rome.

"I have chosen my leader and my fate.

"Which certainly won't be rotting away in a tiny godforsaken village in my sad father's castle.

"March, not rot, for God's sake!"

eight

[the second son flees]

"I am Giovanni Casadio, son of Cosimo Casadio and Valeria Ferrari (who died April 22, 1899).

"I'm thirty-two, and I fled.

"I was in Parma last August, at the barricades. We resisted the fascist attack for two days. They couldn't overtake us alone, those pretend heroes, and so they called the army. The army came, but refused to fight.

"It was a triumph.

"As the blackshirts retreated, I managed to catch a glimpse of my brother Giacomo, the older brother who made me laugh so much as a child imitating the fieldhands.

"I felt an urge to vomit.

"And I fled."

nine

[the third son sketches]

"My name is Gabriele Casadio and I have nothing to do with this whole affair.

"What affair? The one that's about to descend on my family and on Pontescuro.

"I'm already thirty years old and I still haven't found a wife. My father tried his best, as he had done with his other two boys. If you knew how many well-to-do families from every surrounding province came to visit us at the castle, you wouldn't believe it, seeing us still so lost, angry, and alone.

"But my anger, unlike that of my brothers Giacomo and Giovanni, has no need of weapons.

"My anger is a sketchbook. My anger is killing nature with my drawings, my sketches, my studies. That's why I always go walking: to capture every tree or flower, insect or cloud, face or window, light or moon, in the stillness of my crumpled pages.

"I have nothing but those pages to stand up for me, and foreign lands.

"Forget me."

ten

[Dafne Casadio, the fourth child, dies]

"My name is Dafne Casadio and I will forever be twenty-four. I've been dead for seven hours.

"No, not that path, go right. Yes, that way. Be careful, it's slippery. There's no water yet, the river's dams are strong. And even if it might make me glad, making of me what I couldn't become in life, it's not my tears, either. It's the fog, spreading on its way out. Soon it'll be light and someone will find me. With my red ribbon around my neck. That's how I died: with a red ribbon around my neck. Strangled, they'll say. It's not even silk, they'll say. But then again, silk wasn't right for her, that slut.

"That's what they'll say, but low enough so as not to disturb their consciences.

"But what was I, who was I, in life?

"I am the master's last-born. My mother died too soon for me to feel loved. And my father was busy with his business, with no time for affection. I had three older brothers, but they were boys and I wasn't, and this only increased my solitude.

"Many people were in and out of the castle all through my childhood, it's true: my father hadn't put a lock on the front door. The detonator of his strict widowerhood was stuck for a while only to then discharge an unbearable silence, and it was in that very that silence, after repeatedly hearing it from relatives, farmers, and nobles, that I came to believe I was an especially beautiful girl.

"I was blond, like my mother. I had such light in my hair it was almost an affront. It was as if all the earth's vitality, for reasons unknown, had gathered over my brow, leaving everyone else a colorless, foggy landscape.

"I had a high forehead, a straight and well-proportioned nose, and lips as full as necessary, I quickly learned, wanting them and yet keeping the proper distance from them, unless I was the one to give a sign of encouragement.

"My room was spacious and filled with toys, and I had a nanny taking care of me, a woman I have forgotten everything about, even her name.

But I tormented her, this I remember, and I considered her a kind of warden, and in some way responsible for my mother's death.

The 'Three Gs," as I began to call my brothers, ignored me with the ferocity of which especially boys are capable, and so, as soon as I gained confidence and consciousness of my appearance, which was quite early, I assure you, I repaid it with a silent violence even more unbearable than theirs had been.

"By fourteen I was no longer governable by familial authority. My father, who had placed in me, the only female exponent of his bloodline, a last grasp at happiness, had no choice but to capitulate in the face of my unruliness. I couldn't spend another minute in the nauseating frilliness of my bedroom nor even in the castle, except to return at night to sleep.

"I began going down to the village every day, first thing in the morning. I would walk slowly to extend the trip beyond just a few minutes along those dirt roads that wound around the hovels that the residents of Pontescuro called houses like a hangman's noose.

"And I knew them, those brutes. It took me over a year to make them head-on enemies, which made things easier, finally. I preferred that. But before... Before, they would steer clear of me, I would hear the creak of closing shutters, women half murmuring a prayer or crossing their deflated or caved in chests.

"The women didn't scare me, I was cognizant of the reasons for their premature decrepitude and the viciousness not even their heavy, restrictive underskirts could contain.

"With the men it was even simpler. Men desired me, but they didn't know what to do about it. No one in Pontescuro is accustomed to having desires. And so I took them by the scruff of that feverish paralysis: those gnarled, sweaty hands stuck in their pockets, those puppy-dog eyes, those stiffened members concealed in shame—all of these things were perfect hooks for me to hang the carcass of the whole village.

"But it had to be butchered first.

"There was an abandoned barn past the last house before the open countryside to the south. No one ever went there because it was on the edge of the unknown, the open road, but especially because it was considered a sinister place, something to do with a generations-old story about a jilted lover and revenge.

"I made it my call house.

"Deep in the night, on the day of my sixteenth birthday, I let in through the back, through the dusty brick opening, the gift I had decided to give myself: my first peasant.

"His name was Gené and he was shaking like a leaf. He came back other times, but he had to wait his turn.

"After a few months, as I was saying, the village began to scorn me to my face. And maybe if they were even slightly intelligent, they would've been able to tell from the one dopey grin, always the same expression but every day on a different face, who'd been the latest to unbuckle his belt. But no one ever thought to follow me, and no one ever thought of the sinister barn.

"I couldn't have cared less if the talk about me somehow made its way up the street through the open door to the castle where my father had buried himself and planted itself before his despair, organized in the perfectly tabulated columns of his ledger books. In fact, that was probably what I wanted. And it almost certainly happened. But I never took the trouble to find out. Rather, at some point I discovered that I was more interested in figuring out the reason for my behavior, given that I was the one who started it, without anyone ever having harmed the master's little girl, or without that little girl turned maneater having found anything better than the repulsion and disgust that she felt once her legs were closed again.

"I didn't figure out much, but I reconsidered the life choices of my three brothers. When it came down to it, wasn't I too trying to escape just like them? Except that my escape didn't require me to relocate, and besides, I never would have been able to link up with a bunch of fanatics or join the army, let alone sleep in ditches, living out in the open and talking to the trees, becoming a drifter as I heard Gabriele had. An archangel idiot, that hapless brother of mine.

"No, I had to stay here at my father's side. I was the woman of the family. I was the substitute for my mother. I was living proof of our fated disgrace.

"I just chose not to accept it."

eleven

[Don Antonio hooked]

"I went to mass on Sunday morning, just like everyone else, or almost. My father didn't go out for that occasion either. The town would have been shocked to see him, but not as shocked as every time they saw me.

"Their shock, their indignation, as their certainty of being in the right, at Jesus' side in a silent march of compassion, that false compassion put on so disgustingly in their conviction of being the elect, the just, never left their faces upon my entrance in that cold damp hovel that was the Pontescuro church.

"But even there, there was always at least one man lowering his gaze to the floor, usually the last one to have sprinkled his foul holy water on my belly.

"But no one could do anything about it. No one could make me change my ways, prevent me from taking the host in my mouth and crushing it between my teeth with a bitterness only I could taste.

"One Sunday morning a few years later, when I had just turned twenty-two, a new priest appeared at the altar. The farmers and their wives were enchanted with his homily that morning, and while everyone hung on the new pastor's every word, I was thinking about how to hook him myself.

"After all, he was a man too; the only thing he had different from the others was the number of buttons to undo.

"His name was Don Antonio."

twelve

[the new priest turns the key to oblivion]

"My name is still Don Antonio, I am a young priest.

"I was born in Padua and my parents baptized me in honor of that Portuguese Franciscan, Anthony of Padua—at least I think so. My family was noble, my father a descendant of Godfrey of Bouillon, King of Jerusalem, and so my upbringing was forged by taking up arms. Yet my fate held an entirely different type of crusade. But not Jerusalem—they sent me from the upper echelon down to Pontescuro. And for what? To save some tramp and take away her powers, since everyone in the village said she was a witch and had stolen the husbands' sanity, shriveled the wives' breasts, and struck the children and animals with mysterious maladies. And so on.

"But what did they want from me? What did they expect in Rome, those pearl-clutchers? And these poor laborers here, these families subjugated by the very powers from which they begged for freedom? That an Inquisitor would swoop in and restore justice and peace? Well, they were wrong. They had to settle for a man.

"There was only one person in the whole village who had no complaints about who I really was: Dafne Casadio. She knew how to get past the cassock, plumb my throbbing doubt, and turn it into treasure, no doubt, though I too benefited from her technique.

"But why, I wondered in the early days of my transfer, did they choose me to pacify the silent rebellion of an entire village? Why me, to subdue collective superstition and soothe a soul devoted to evil? Perhaps my superiors weren't aware that I don't believe in the devil, and had no inkling—of course they didn't, I'd kept it well hidden—that, based on the conclusions I'd come to at the end of my studies, with a clear head, I never would have attributed to any soul an immanent capacity for evil?

"Man is born with the loss of knowledge; in fact, I'm convinced that our entry into the world is ushered not by human hands or the tools of the trade, but unlocked with the key of oblivion. It is a prerequisite: losing a general sense of human history and what came before it; forgetting having known everything, having been part of it from our first cry. Without that, we are not born.

"So tell me, how could a creature thrust into life, riven and torn from eternity and stripped of memory, have some absolute consciousness of evil? Or of good, for that matter?

"I could have rebelled against my family when I was young and taken up a military career, but that idea was what actually led me to enter the seminary. Because I had true compassion and an absence of judgment. Because I could look people in the eyes and understand them, not judge them. Had they discovered this, I would have been excommunicated. But it was such a well-kept secret that I wound up on the holier side of the altar in a crumbling little church in a foggy backwater. Ponderously delivering sermons of reassurance.

"To banish evil! I encouraged those poor souls every Sunday.

"While by night I sucked at its teat."

thirteen

[the fog observes the end]

"Their names were Giovanni, Tonio, Puccio, Giorgione, Luigi, Mario. Their names were Guglielmetto, Rico, Luciano, Paolo di Ca' Bassa, Michelino, Paolo di Ca' Alta. And then there were Franchino, Enrico, Gené, Bandiera, who was in fact a man despite his unique name ending in a feminine A. There were still others, but deep down, none of them were real men. With one yawn I could swallow them all, me with my weak feminine name.

"I was certainly neither the only one nor was I the most driven. The fog recedes at some point, and so I did. But Dafne never went away. She spent all of her time confirming what she already knew, what she had always known.

"And while they tried in vain to soften the force of their palms pressed against her breasts, and practically tore the garters off of stockings stained with dirt and wine, and lowered underwear made of thick, rough cloth, and attempted to transform frantic gobbling into decent kisses or at least something with a margin of grace or gratitude, two elements of life they'd never known nor had the slightest idea how to express. And while Giovanni, Tonio, Puccio, Giorgione, Luigi, and Mario were groping and fumbling, pressing and spreading, and while Guglielmetto, Rico, Luciano, Michelino, and the Paolos di Ca' Bassa and di Ca' Alta gulped and cursed their seed the way one would a premature harvest that will bring sadness for an entire season, Dafne knew that soon she would reach a full gallop, she was well on her way, from below, from beyond the horizon's edge, and she proceeded without tiring, without pauses, without stops, in the dark and in the bastard light, in the dripping cold and still air, yes, she, paralyzed in her den, motionless.

"The end continued down its perfect path."

fourteen

[the fog meets the jay]

"But these lands, take it from someone who has always inhabited them from above, are like a mix of dreams, and when you open your eyes you don't know whether you feel frightened and threatened by mysterious forces or like the uncontested master of your life and destiny.

"That's not so with any open countryside, as you may be thinking. Some are geometric, drawn with ruler and square, some are wavy and fluffy like cotton candy, and still others, lazy and yawning, are devoid of character.

"The countryside surrounding Pontescuro, just beyond the barn, is a long series of unraveled threads, things headed toward new solutions.

"Running along the sides of the one street are deep ditches, and the farmworkers will try to tell you they're for irrigation or rainwater, the occasional motorists that they're subject to the whims of the vehicle or fatigue: those irrigation ditches are nothing more than the deep imprint of the ultimate spirit of the place, its signature.

"In the early morning I love to stretch out in those ditches, heedless of the water, while the fields begin to awaken into their own special limbo, outstretching their clods of dirt from down below, awaiting the man to come with the ox, both of the two ruminating the toil of another day identical to the one before, the former propelled by a breakfast of bread soaked in a glass of the light red sparkling wine they make in these parts, and the latter by the mirage of new, more succulent grass.

"But the man is mistaken, and the ox is mistaken, and under the creaky planks taking them into the fields, the water, only apparently still, will roll laughing down to the mouth of silence, where road, field, and ditches merge in a single blur.

"Every so often I see the new priest's billowing vestments around the corner of the barn like a tongue of black fire, a slash, an affront to the calm air of the landscape, at an hour too early for matins, or a home blessing, or a courtesy call; and that barn is nothing but ghosts and bugbears, superstitions and creaks—nothing that would appear to concern a young clergyman.

"But here in Pontescuro I know appearances are an illusion, because appearances are nothing: life itself, in other words, its slipping past undisturbed, like Dafne now smoothing her dress and emerging from the shadow of the brick wall, rosy and smiling, absolved.

"I'm not the only one watching her. There are the groves of field maples in the distance, and the elm trees, and even a few mulberry trees, fanning out at the wind's open mouth, its indignation. These are trees that have been grown for centuries, mostly for ornament or defining property lines, as no one around here has the gift of foresight and those who did appreciate the landscape left as soon as they could, like Casadio's sons did.

"The Apennines aren't accessible on foot, but they are by wing. And so I made a friend. When I first saw her here I could hardly believe it.

"What is this flying palette of color doing in a gray place like this? I know her, I know her usual spots. I would see her on my way down from the mountains, winding through the woods into the valley. The forest was her home, and it was inside those humid confines, in that shadowy green lattice, that she would poke her beak and zip through the few strips of open air with her ruddy plumage of wing feathers and tail feathers, blue covert feathers and white throat.

"She's a jay. She must have been driven to Pontescuro by hunger, attracted by the warm draft of all those poor folks' chimneys.

"We keep each other company at dawn, and since she is able to communicate with me, I know exactly where she came from, I know the easterly place she left behind.

"Not everyone can speak the language of fog.

"She's a mimic."

fifteen

[the jay weighs the consequences]

"Gené is crying in bed, touching himself under the covers, not knowing why he feels like he's suffering and feels happy too, these aren't two distinct feelings, they go together, caw, caw, and he doesn't know how to choose between being content or sad, what to believe with the whole tumult that's rising in his head, they're thoughts, just thoughts, caw, caw, but thoughts... Gené doesn't even know what thoughts are.

"Don Antonio pairs up his thoughts the way he does with his silk slippers in the evening, which he brought from the East along with some Moroccan leather missals and vestments, and nothing bothers him when he emerges from his clean-smelling sheets, not even the thought of losing Dafne, because sooner or later he will, that much is certain, just as he'll lose the town and the church and the men and women who come to him, asking him to drive the girl out of the community, and for a brief moment Don Antonio becomes like Gené: a confused little man, caw, caw, someone who can identify the place for justice and the place for happiness, only to discover that they are enemy fortresses, that there will be no way to compromise, forge peace, and lay down their arms, but it only lasts for a moment, and by the time his feet slip into the soft fabric it's already over.

"There's no difference between Cosimo Casadio's canopy and his castle, caw caw, he gets lost in both, they're both too vast, now that he only has servants around, now that his family is entirely contained in the ledgers and the cargo of the boats down at the river, and that's it, nothing more, his wife and children are lost between an earthly voyage and madness, between death and political allegiance, between a sketchbook and an overwhelming horizon devoid of life. Every time he wakes up, he counts the shadowy corners, the imprints of loss, starting with the pillow beside him, and then proceeds to waste another day, his head down.

"Giovanni and Tonio and Puccio are also very good at wasting their days, caw, caw. Giorgione swears loudly, announcing, 'Hey, you cretins, I'm awake!'. I can almost hear him saying it, but it's only in my head, I know the language of man, and he's just propping himself up, nothing more, just like the two Paolos, di Ca' Alta who's up earlier than usual as today is his turn with Dafne so long as she doesn't change her mind, and di Ca' Bassa announcing to his wife that he's going with Ca' Alta to the washhouse and then going to the field, and his wife looks at him surprised and suspicious, she knows he wants to keep his eyes busy, see what the mood is like out there, caw, caw.

"Bandiera comes up with rationales for vendettas before he even turns on the light in the morning, but once the light is on he doesn't realize that with a name that means "flag" if he started traveling a little he'd make all kinds of friends indeed, caw, caw. They'd give him a black shirt, no one would dream of calling him a faggot or an invert, I could fly over his rooftop and tell him but he wouldn't understand me; he doesn't even understand other men.

"And so, men stay in bed and I stay in the air.

"I can cover great distances in one day; fact is, I've gotten used to Pontescuro, and if I left, it would make the fog sad, which would make the town even sadder.

"I stay because I know how to weigh consequences and because there is one person, just one, in Pontescuro who knows my caw, caw.

"He's my walking buddy.

"Because of me, the town started calling him Ciaccio. Caw, caw."

sixteen

[the river tells Ciaccio's story]

"When they found him, it was a summer morning in 1899. He licked my cheek and laughed. He was wrapped in a heavy, dirty, wool cloth, through an oval opening of which emerged a wonderstruck little face and a tiny arm that had somehow managed to free itself from the cloth and was pointing toward the nearest tree. It was just a shrub—I am nearly bare—but the baby laughed and looked at it the way we might at an unexpected visitor who brings us wonderful news, like a good and generous giant. The sunlight was beginning to penetrate the stones, blending with that breeze that follows wherever I pass. Everything was perfect and silent, and the baby seemed to be aware of it too.

"Then again, I'm an adult and I've learned to remain calm. Nothing scares or ruffles me any longer. The era of my tumultuous youth is long gone, countless provinces and human footsteps away. I was, and am still to some, a frail newborn, or a daredevil, troublemaking kid, or a stocky, lazy young man. And further along, I know I will be, and for some already am, an old man who lingers over his story, taking his time, maybe just to make it last another bend or two.

"I am the river, and I am the only one who can tell Ciaccio's story from the beginning.

"Ciaccio, obviously, when they found him and took him away, had no name.

"He was left there by a girl I had never seen before. She came from the city, riding a bicycle unsteadily, with one eye on the road and one on the basket nestled between the handlebars with the little bundle inside.

"She looked about sixteen or seventeen years old, and despite the hellfire in her eyes and the strands of black hair sticking to her sweaty brow, there survived a streak of beauty that someone must have already dampened, but not extinguished.

"She stopped at the point where I bend and sneak through Pontescuro, got off the bicycle, and with it leaning on her hip, she gingerly removed the baby from his protective basket, and then, letting the bike fall to the ground, she looked at me and came over.

"I thought she wanted to drown the baby, or at least abandon it to my womb, gentler and more hospitable than hers, and already I poised myself to find a way to dissuade her, maybe asking for help from the wind in the trees or a bird's warning call—some kind of sign that, in short, I was certain, she would have taken as a prompt to desist and take the child back home. Then she spotted a dilapidated, abandoned rowboat behind some sparse vegetation about 50 steps away on her right.

"She went over and examined it carefully, and holding the newborn in the crook of her arm, she bent down and with her free hand began to uproot the humble vegetation that had grown around it, piling it on the blades of grass that poked through the gaps between the rotted planks.

"She cleared enough of the surface to lay the bundle on it. With both her arms free, she went on ripping out the plants while the daylight very timidly peeked out from the short horizon on my other shore.

"Planting one foot as leverage, and summoning all of the strength she had left in her body, she managed to pull the side of the boat towards the shore past what must have once been the water line so that the unusual white package could be spotted even from far away. Then she crouched down, with her back to me, and muttered a few distinct phrases to the baby, who smiled in response, and then she turned, went back to the bicycle, got on, and rode off.

"The new day peeled away from the sky, and two jays took wing from the leafy branches in the distance.

"I knew those birds. They didn't care for open spaces, never came near inhabited areas, at least back then, and didn't even trust me.

"However, on that occasion they came out of the thicket and headed straight for the tiny castoff, landing a few steps away.

"'Caw, caw,' said the birds.

"'Caw, caw,' said the baby."

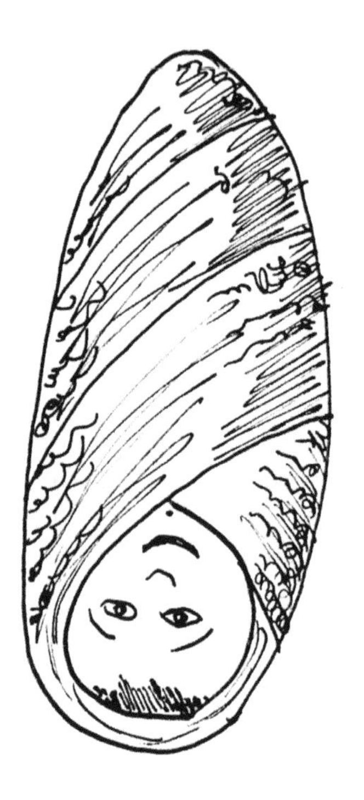

seventeen

[Làinfondo begs for wine and finds a baby]

Not thirty minutes later, on that summer morning in 1899, coming from the same direction from where the jays had appeared, Làinfondo happened by and found the baby

Làinfondo was a man without a past. Of an indefinite age between thirty and fifty, he was absolutely unable to solve the mystery of his own birth.

"As for being born, I was born. What do you care about the rest?" That was the most articulate description he ever expressed, even if only with his eyes.

The truth was, Làinfondo was unable to respond to any question he was asked. The purpose of his mouth was above all to hold up the half-rusted edge of a paint can he secured around his neck with a filthy rope.

Decked out thus, he would go around town, knocking on doors with his effective and straightforward method: going from the first house to the last. Then he would wait patiently for someone to open the door.

Generally it was a woman or an elderly person, as all the able-bodied men were in the fields or at the docks.

They came to know him and after a while, he became less and less likely to come across a door that remained closed to him, except for the castle. Because there was always someone who stayed home.

Houses aren't left vacant, not even for a few hours. A house is the only sure thing, those women and old folks would tell him, while he, with a silent, toothless grin, sharply extended an arm, and the can of paint nearly reached their chin. Then they would reprimand him, every time, even if they already knew his reaction.

"And you," they pressed, "where is your house, where exactly do you live?" and before taking the can and shutting the door in his face, going to the kitchen for some old wine and pouring it in that wretch's cup, then returning and opening the door back up again and holding it out to him like the uppity folks who show off their generous offerings in church every Sunday, they would wait for the man to roll out his entire vocabulary, which they enjoyed more than pay day.

He must have known it. Somehow, he perceived the expectation and even if he wanted to, wouldn't have been able to do anything different. And so he would turn three-quarters, stare toward a hazy area near the river past the last houses of Pontescuro, and with the arm his cup forgot, point to a spot immersed in the light mist of the plain where the horizon met the low clouds, and say: "Làinfondo." Down there.

No one, ever, had ever heard him speak any other words. Then he would take his wine and go off happily to the next dwelling.

And so, in time, everyone began to call him Làinfondo, and when he showed up, for those peasants it was like the traveling circus had come to the door.

That summer morning in 1899, Làinfondo didn't make anyone laugh.

In Ca' Bassa, at the last house before the fields and the first one that anyone coming from the fields or the river passes by, Paolo's grandmother, Mrs. Bartolini, as soon as she heard that knock on the door, deeming it a little harder than usual, appeared at the door ready with a bottle of wine in her hand.

But at the sight of this poor man and his onerous new accessory, she wasn't sure what to do next.

Had that weirdo stolen a baby? Should she scream and call for help? Or overcome her repulsion, grab him by his raggedy sleeve and pull him inside?

Who was that infant? Where did it come from? What needed to be done?

She certainly couldn't ask Làinfondo, who was standing there with even more fear in his expression than her and wouldn't answer anyway, and so, in that interval of uncertainty, it was the baby's smile to decide.

eighteen

[feeding a new mouth]

They took him to the castle, to Master Cosimo, who had money and rooms, but he wanted no part of it.

He said that bloodlines are a serious matter, and to give one's name to a descendant outside one's own isn't something any respectable person would do.

Those people should deal with it themselves, even though they treated the animals like children and their children like animals. Weren't they all on his payroll anyway?

He knew exactly how much he shelled out for each family, and there was plenty to feed one more mouth, and if absolutely no one would to take him, this child of the horizon, they could come together and arrange for each family to take care of him a month at a time.

The men had gone there dressed up and clean shaven and the women were groomed and perfumed, and that was the last time one could speak of a common goal in Pontescuro for many years to come.

Unity wouldn't be restored until Cosimo Casadio's year-old daughter, pampered in the castle parlor like the princess of the world, was grown enough to develop breasts.

Cosimo, despite not really believing them, used strong words to extricate himself from the Pontescuro delegation as quickly as possible. Yet they, burying their indignation and offense, took his suggestion to heart, and so for a few years the little one was passed from house to house: a smiling bundle wrapped in bigger and bigger scraps of cloth.

No one in the village, not even the elderly, worried about giving him a proper upbringing and a happy childhood. What did the angels, cherubim, Mother Mary and kin expect? Was he not the child of nothing, come from nothing, brought there by Làinfondo, who was less than nothing?

Làinfondo, in the meantime, had resumed his routine of knocking on doors, wine weighing down the tin can around his neck, and his arm pointing "over there" and making the women laugh with his contagious phrase: "Làinfondo!"

But in the evenings when he found himself alone by the rotted boat, his spirit soothed by the gentle sloshing of wine in his belly, he would kneel on the grass once pulled out by young female hands and now grown back as if nothing had ever happened, and wait for the strange thing to take over his face.

Làinfondo drank, kneeled, and cried, while the little child in the village grew, laughed, and awaited a name.

Everyone remembered what their master had said, and in some way, turned it around in their favor.

That they treated their children like beasts of burden was certainly an unfair accusation, but they understood very well why Casadio had made it: if you fail to fulfill a duty, make everyone else feel more negligent than you and everything will be fine.

Didn't the whole village work that way, when it came down to it?

They were poor, but not stupid, and docile only because of the old rule: a dog mustn't eat its master's prey.

Nevertheless, they still couldn't give him a name, as he was not their son.

"Your name is a gift that sticks to you," was the first statement made when they met to decide what to do in the muddy clearing by the bridge, the only scrap of ground they had resembling a town square.

"He's right," someone else remarked. "Take a look at us, we're Tratáur, Arsantéla, Barbet, Vipra, Sreza..."

"What does that have to do with it," commented the mother of Rico, someone who, twenty years later, could only take Dafne if he pushed her head down until she vanished in the hay. She went on, in a mean voice: "Those are the names we called each other because of something we did, and lived up to them by keeping on doing whatever it was when we were older. But in this case it's a baby who hasn't done anything yet, he's too little, no? How else can I explain it to you?"

And then along came the long-awaited opinion of Michelino's uncle, whom everyone called Furàza, clam, because he always showed up to take on the nasty and worst part of a job and the meager wages and the boss's excessive demands, but nothing got to him, the others would crack first, and he, safe inside his shell, without causing harm to anyone, like a clam, and Michelino's uncle, Furàza, spitting on the ground in order to demand complete silence, said that the baby actually did do something, one thing only, just like his idiot foundling father, Làinfondo.

One of them asked for a drink, the other to hold him, who laughed and pointed at the sky making his funny little cry

Everyone realized on the spot that Furàza had found him his name.

nineteen

[the apprenticeship of Ciaccio and Dafne]

Ciaccio, growing up, wanted for rooms.

Unlike Dafne, he didn't have a playroom all to himself, much less someone by his side always ready to fulfill his every desire.

He had to content himself with kitchens, propped on the table next to the flour while the women cursed the too-low flame and how much longer it took to cook the polenta; when the men came back home for a break, their eyes heavy with rage and haste, they wanted to dig in right away.

Ciaccio didn't complain, but he didn't have any fun, either.

Because in each family that received him for a few weeks it was always the same: different rooms, steam from the stove and their breath, and far more curses than smiles.

Dafne, despite being overwhelmed with toys, never complained either, and likewise knew nothing of happiness.

All she knew was that, aside from her brothers, she couldn't be around other children; she wasn't allowed to, it was dangerous, they told her.

Were her dolls not a special kind of children? So obedient that they would say all the right words without a single complaint and move exactly how she wanted? They respected her, and a child who commands respect, her father had taught her, means being important, a child who is a leader, who once grown, will make their way in the world. Dafne was confused: for one thing she wasn't the leader, because she came after Giacomo, Giovanni, and Gabriele, three boys who were permitted to play outside, as long as they remained in sight, whereas she, like all of the girls in Pontescuro, had to stay inside. It didn't matter if she lived like a princess, as they kept telling her, because she was still a girl, and Sunday mass and holidays were the only occasions she could go out. How was she supposed to make her way in the world if all of the roads were closed to her?

Ciaccio, at the age of twelve, in 1911, was left with Bandiera's father, Emilio by baptism but Zuntura by life, known as the fix-it man of the village, who could repair anything from wobbly plows to busted teeth.

He'd been left a widower, as was soon to befall Mr. Casadio, and while the master of the waters would shut himself inside his vast, well-heated castle, Emilio found comfort in his back house, a refuge he'd built himself piece by piece out of logs, corrugated sheet metal, and scrap material that the villagers gave him in exchange for his service. He called it "the laboratory," and everyone else, in a whisper, "the pigsty."

As a widower, he preferred staying in there over the house, the kitchen, and especially the bedroom. He had even put bed slats in there and covered the slack mesh with a board so hard it justified a sleep that would be better called insomnia.

Zuntura almost never left his laboratory, at least until the village decided to present him with an apprentice, Ciaccio.

"Don't worry about the expense," they had told him. "We'll bring him food, and you'll put a roof over his head, even if it is metal, and you'll put something sensible and practical in his head, too. Get him to learn something, Emilio. Who, better than you, could teach him about life?"

The boy had little reason to object; if anything, there was a new twinkle in his smiling eyes when he saw his new house. Partly because a shack erected in the freedom of an untended lawn was better than walls, a breeze better than a closed window; and a piece of metal more delicate than a brick roof—the birds could be heard walking on top of it. And also because that man, Zuntura, in just a few square meters, had managed to fit in a pile of sickles, hand-forged nails, hoes, keys, brass weights, a wagon wheel, iron scissors, hooks of various sizes, a drawknife, wooden box graters, winches, pliers, rakes, and billhooks, buckets and bed warmers, a couple of ladders, coffee roasters and lanterns, a butter churn, scrapers and scales, brass vises and jaw spreaders, little tools for mysterious uses lying on a workbench, and also string of various thicknesses and colored ribbon—lots of string and ribbon.

Ciaccio loved them.

By the age of twelve, Dafne, unable to change the words of the grown-ups, had begun to govern the life and death of her little dolls.

She tore off their clothes, rolled them up carefully, and then cut them into little strips of fabric that she used to hang them from the backs of chairs and under her precious inlaid desk.

The respective apprenticeships of the two children were long and secret, but the seasons passed over them in a flash.

twenty

[the village idiot and the strips of fabric]

The good thing about the wise is that they open the fences and let others in when they need to be let in, and let them out when they need to be let out.

This is a teaching forged for interior occurrences, but is perfectly applicable to everyday life.

If you had to pick out a wise man in Pontescuro, it would be Emilio, aka Zuntura, who had taken up compiling a rulebook of behavior, with Ciaccio as the model.

He answered all his questions about the different tools, and while he realized that the boy would forget all about the billhook or the dental pliers as soon as he stepped outside to the open air and the trees with his pockets full of strings and ribbons, Zuntura was discovering the immense evocative power of some of the objects, and their secret uses, once arranged in the little house.

For this reason, Emilio wasn't too insistent with the boy and his evidently dull intellect: that evidence was misleading.

Just as a forgotten object continues to absorb its past actions, while Emilio relived all the repairs he'd made in his mind: the smiles, the way the houses smelled, the prayers and the worries of the villagers, Ciaccio too only assimilated the connection between his master's words and the inert materials he was talking about when he was finally able to go stretch out in the fields, gulping the air with giant yawns.

Ciaccio wasn't stupid–on the contrary: he simply had his own way of interpreting space, perhaps like that of birds, which had become his friends.

His gaze took in the open expanse, the empty blue, and rarely directed downward, whereas everyone else in Pontescuro, with the exception of Emilio, kept their eyes on the ground, now out of love now out of resentment, content to keep to themselves without knowing how to articulate it.

Ciaccio, on the other hand, wanted to find harmony with everything that was free, with all the elements that lacked a specific function, yet, as he felt vaguely, gave him a sense of what he truly was: an orphan boy in a poor village of people who were just trying to get by. The river water and the clouds, tree bark, morning fog, leaves, wings, the horizon: the ingredients of life. The horizon wasn't the bar of a locked cage and the sky wasn't a lid over his head. He could be happy on eyesight alone.

Another thing that he had realized growing up was that the men and women of Pontescuro needed to see misfortune, misery, and stupidity oppressing others, and as long as the village remained standing, it was by their bitter sweat. But it was missing an idiot, and as the months and years went by, Ciaccio wound up filling that vacancy.

There were some advantages to being the village idiot and to having a putative father who could see inside and through appearances. He could leave the shack and run wherever he wanted without the peasants in the distance pointing fingers. There was no such thing as bizarre behavior because he was the village idiot, he knew his rights.

And he left everyone in peace. He didn't go knocking on any doors like Làinfondo begging for wine, or insulting anyone who came within earshot, as the rich man's daughter had begun to do, without even going door to door.

When she—her name was Dafne, he'd been told—turned seventeen, she had gifted herself the pleasure of scorning the women and debilitating the men, especially the ones who were preparing to leave for war.

In the spring of 1915, Ciaccio—he had been told this too—being sixteen and having the fortune of being an idiot, didn't have to go to war.

Not that it made much difference to him—he didn't understand men very well no matter where he was, except Zuntura, of course, and now, he thought, Dafne, who to him seemed very sweet and not a wicked temptress, even though he had never spoken to her.

During the war years, Ciaccio would tie strips of cloth around tree branches with slow, meticulous gestures, and given the abruptly decreased population in the fields, undisturbed.

Maybe he would have tied them around gun barrels or severed limbs in the trenches, who knows? He never knew how to respond to the women in the evenings when they said, "Go take your string to tie around my son's ankles and bring him back home, the trenches are a death sentence."

He asked about it one morning, his eyes lowered sheepishly, and Emilio told him what a trench was and what a war was, all the while filling him a wooden crate with leftover straps and cords, ribbons and gauze, laces from unpaired shoes and unraveled hems, and Ciaccio fell asleep hugging that crate—it was his precious treasure chest, and with its contents he could talk to the natural world, be part of it. Caw, caw.

When the war was over, to the soldiers who returned on their own two legs, no sooner than they had brushed their mothers' warm cheeks or looked from the abyss in their eyes to the blank gazes of their fathers, it was evident that peace was hiding a lot past the horizon of those plots of land. Rural life was in tumult.

The peasant farmers were striking, and the workers' movements had reached Pontescuro, where there were no large estates, but families, decimated by the conflict, were demanding that landowners hire more wage laborers.

Cosimo Casadio responded by requesting prompt intervention from Rome, and Rome sent squadristi to quell the rebellion. It worked in a flash: Pontescuro was a speck compared to the vast parcels of the south, and accommodating the petty lord of a speck was the least of the Fascists' priorities. They did the essential minimum, because after all, Casadio's river transports were still needed for the Fascist cause, but it all ended in a few days.

Ciaccio resumed adorning tree branches and trunks with new ribbons, since the blackshirts had removed them before they left (what was that provocation, those colors, all that red in the fields?) and sometimes Dafne came along to keep him company.

There they were, side by side, in silence. She unraveled the tangled ball of string, he took them from her one by one, smiling and looking into her eyes, then he tied a knot and sang, tied and sang.

Seen from afar they resembled a painting that had magically come to life. One of those paintings hung in the important galleries in the big cities.

One day, Nella, the town gossip, with her rapid, hobbling gait, burst into that painting.

twenty-one

[Don Andreino, the old priest, Nella, the maid, and their appetites]

Before Don Antonio, coming to town in 1920, demoted Nella to bothersome background figure, just one of the many lamentatious and discontented voices he heard in church and in the street when he went out dragging the hem of his vestments, Nella had been an authority in the Pontescuro religious circle, for she was the housemaid for the old parish priest, Don Andreino.

Don Andreino had two virtues and an unspecified number of defects that were so well hidden everyone in town adored him. One of his most admired qualities in Pontescuro was, first and foremost, the fact that he had been born there, a trait not at all trivial or to be taken for granted given that his predecessors, according to both memory and record, originated from other locales evidently more generous in terms of vocation, a tradition that would be carried on, and by a city priest, no less, with the figure of Don Antonio.

Unlike Don Antonio, Don Andreino's vocation wasn't developed by poring over the canonical texts by candlelight with his head down and his index finger following every line, but with his entire hand closed around a ladle lifted like an aspergillum by the light of the wood stove blessing the advent of polenta.

In fact, the priest's second virtue was contained in his name, whose diminutive defined the size of its owner by antithesis, who from the age of thirteen had gained 10 kilos every year of his life.

When it was time for his assignment as priest, after finishing seminary forkful by forkful, Don Andreino weighed 110 kilos, give an Ave Maria take an Ora Pro Nobis, and this characteristic, rather than bothering the indigent inhabitants of Pontescuro, melted their hearts and cashed in on their faith. Anyone who eats that much has nothing to hide, they figured. Anyone who stuffs himself and smiles at the pot has a heart that's free and pure, they figured. Anyone who feasts on breads and trimmings knows how to clear a murky soul, they figured. Anyone ready to fill his gullet at any hour of the day or night knows the straight way and is steady on our life's journey, the inhabitants of Pontescuro had figured.

But they figured wrong, because it was precisely in those moments, at the end of his morning, afternoon, or evening meals that Don Andreino's array of shortcomings emerged.

The first to notice them, and to keep them to herself for her own personal gain, was Ornella, who lived in the house past the mulberry tree and, being of marrying age but without suitors, had been picked out by Don Andreino for a future housekeeping position.

Her family, all too happy to reduce the number of daily meals on their table, handed her over to him along with a potato and nettle pie in gratitude.

Nella was in fact almost as hearty an eater as the priest, and that communion of the palate, from his first days in office, had revealed to her that the phrase, "anyone who eats that much..." ended not with "has nothing to hide," but rather with "will have a great thirst in his soul."

Her fellow villagers had been mistaken, it didn't take long for her to realize, but she was fine with their error since Don Andreino, as a man of the church, had proved to be quite generous in sharing with her pours of golden Vin Santo and tastings from brimful bottles of entirely secular Rubizzo, the best they had in town—they wouldn't have given him anything less.

Those who eat in excess also drink in excess, and their appetites don't stop there. Just enough time to get comfortable and then it happened.

No one would have imagined, as the evening darkness fell, the priest and his assistant turning into two massive trembling shadows ready to devour each other and meld into one amorphous moaning creature. But the unimaginable often comes true.

Ornella, the plump girl who went to bake bread for the whole town and then load it on her imposing shoulders, almost shamefully, as carrying so much weight was men's work; Nella, who tried to make herself useful to the community by delivering the mail once a month, a superfluous job considering that hardly anyone wrote to those forsaken souls, and had missed by a hair the vacancy for village idiot because it had to be male, had finally succeeded in her goal to replace her misery with a semblance of married life.

She washed the sacred vestments and the profane linens, she dusted the humble makeshift furniture in the tiny rooms, and as best she could kept polished and shiny the room that with a great deal of imagination could be considered a suitable refuge for a savior of souls.

She had even decided to memorize a few key passages from the Gospels, with the assistance of Don Andreino, and she would have succeeded, if in the evenings, always on the pastor's initiative, the fondling and drinking hadn't drowned them in the whirlpools of oblivion.

Yet Nella wasn't entirely happy.

Now that she was the chosen bride of a minister of the Word, she was obliged to keep such a fortune to herself, while it would have added an additional layer of enjoyment to her pleasure to throw it in the faces of the girls who were married or taken, and to their men too, and the elderly women, who had forgotten, perhaps the children too, that they ought to hurry up and do something if they didn't want to get pushed into the ground like insects.

That was just how Nella the chubby girl slowly became Nella the busybody: gossip, tongue-wagging, direct insult and outright cruelty became her outlet, her hydraulic system for disposing of bile, defiling everyone else.

Until one day, her stammering step and wicked tongue were disrupted by the treacherous intrusion of Sergio in the rectory, who wanted to ask Don Andreino a certain favor for the sermon the following Sunday and, having entered without knocking, found the priest receiving the falsetto supplication from Nella's wide-open mouth.

The two composed themselves toppling ciboria, cruets, and chalices, and the intruder returned out into the open without a single word, but the incident had resounding consequences.

In Pontescuro, Sergio was a lifeline, but not the rescuing kind.

Cosimo Casadio ruled the economy of the entire town from above, yet certainly would never dirty his boots personally going to check on field after field, instead assigning this duty to the farmer who seemed the sharpest and most competent, and had trained him so that everyone fell in line under his control.

Sergio had become the steward of Pontescuro.

He was no longer a peasant like the other farmers, but was also nowhere near having a seat at the master's table. He oversaw the field work and reported back, having become a middleman between contempt and frustration.

His numerous offspring hadn't managed to endow him with humanity, but unlike Nella, the resentment that enveloped him was rarely expressed; his outlet was much less vulgar than that of his female counterpart.

He held back his desire to make others suffer with cold hard reasoning, and thanks to his secret evening habit of documenting life in the town in a notebook kept under his pillow, he was able to wait impassively for just the right moment to strike, without forgetting a single episode.

Furthermore, despite not breaking his back loading logs onto boats or kissing the ground from morning to night, Sergio had maintained a slim figure, and in keeping with the collective theory of wineskin bellies versus caved-in bellies, that had to mean he was guarding some dark secrets, and whatever they were, they consumed him like a colony of leeches. So one could imagine what an unexpected surplus of infected blood began pooling in his chest when he discovered the blasphemous affair.

In turn, Nella, silencing the tearful mea culpas of Don Andreino with a finger on his lips, instead of repenting and going back to being the timid bread and post girl, expanded her repertoire of insults, and now was unrestrained on the roads and in the fields, bedraggled like a devil hurling insults: cuckold, sucker, heathen.

And she was preparing to do the same, years later, older and heavier, when she burst onto the insufferable pastoral landscape made by the painted of fools: the master's whoring daughter and Ciaccio who talked to the birds, side by side, in the middle of a field.

She couldn't stand it. Because it had been in the middle of a field during the town winter festival that Sergio had come up to her specifically and described in full detail what he had seen in the rectory with his own eyes, at the beginning of that year, 1913, on his way to the presbytery to request a sacred reading, and discovered a sacred atrocity.

twenty-two

[Zuntura, Ciaccio, and the tools of life]

The curate was removed, and Nella was left without wine, without a missal to study, without blessed food or secrets to keep.

Don Antonio set off on his journey to Pontescuro, unaware of the real reason for his sudden transfer, at least for the time being.

An unusual indolence came over the inhabitants of Pontescuro, almost as if the dirty laundry Sergio had publicly aired had transformed into a collective indulgence of souls.

This remission derived from the maintenance of discipline, which ultimately, however, was only the surface patina of discontented people. People who had replaced the impossibility of enjoying life with the thought that said enjoyment would sooner or later have been repaid in the currency of damnation. But what damnation, now that Don Andreino had shown the fallacy of such reasoning?

The effects of all this were felt in the crops, the fields, the docks, the landscape left to fruit, but it didn't last long—just enough for Cosimo Casadio to put rather restrictive measures in place.

Dafne remained idle for some time, which she made use of by getting closer to that strange grinning boy, Ciaccio.

His meekness was imperturbable, even now that people had taken to scowling at him as though his ribbons and solitary walks were hiding particular maledictions.

For Dafne, those malicious looks were enough to provoke a certain fondness, something she never would have expected to feel in Pontescuro.

Zuntura, one morning, noticed that the tools in the shack were veiled with rust. All of them, without exception. In one night. Eight hours had passed since he had last laid his eyes and hands on them, but it was as if for every breath of his wise man's sleep, an unmerciful clockmaker had pushed his waking forward by a year.

Ciaccio's crate was empty, as was his bed.

twenty-three

[the jay knows things from above]

"I know one thing: everything that is lost or that you wanted to forget, the discarded words, the steps not taken, the choices not made and left to fall away or stuffed lifeless and locked in the bottom of a trunk, will emerge one day past the horizon line and take the place of the sun. They burn eyes, foreheads, hands, and won't look anyone in the eye, indiscriminately striking those directly responsible and the others guilty by omission and inattention.

"It's true, I do know how to imitate human voices, but I can do even more. I can make my way into their hearts, into their faulty reasoning—still incomplete, magmatic, shapeless, and untangle it the way my friend Ciaccio does with balls of string before coming here to the field to give them to the trees.

"When it's all laid out, the result isn't pretty.

"That's why I spend more time in the air than on land. The ground isn't firm as it seems; it churns from within, like the hearts of the people of Pontescuro. And at night, when everything is still, the right word isn't peace— the right word remains stuck to the chests heaving with discontent and envy, regret and resentment.

"The right word is always the same: war.

"Look at that woman now. Watch her emerge with all the momentum that her legs allow. Maybe she wanted to be something else, but she doesn't remember anymore. Since she went to the rectory, she doesn't remember.

"Yes, I prefer the sky to the ground. The ground isn't stable, not even in the middle of a plain like this one. Its slopes are phenomenal and miraculous: you can slide along the wall of a gesture, a choice, a chance event without stopping until you hit the ground.

"On the other hand, the air is safe because only the gods can bring down the sky, and gods are nothing but broken wings, accidents.

"Here she comes, hulking and shrieking, heading for the two young people.

"She's broken inside, and you could blame the wine or Don Andreino, the letters that never arrived for anyone, the bread leavened with mockery, the man never found or perhaps was never even born.

"But I want to repeat, like a parrot, a bird unknown to them here, "you don't fall into blame, you slip into it."

"I told you this is a false plain. You slip and get swallowed up. And that is how men are consumed by what they've left unfinished, by the stares of others, even the meticulous, tedious rhythm of the seasons, the harvesting and planting, the mechanism stolen from card players who discard one day and pick up another until someone takes the whole deck, men are swallowed up by all of these things.

"But Nella doesn't have this awareness. She needs to be lighter—not light enough to hover in the air like me, I mean, but just to have the sense that true happiness lies closer to emptiness, it calls for light baggage—a red ribbon, for example.

"All the red Nella has are her hands clawing the air, almost as if she wanted to tear it away from the two kids, while sputtering still inaudible words.

"Red are the bellows of her cheeks, and the handkerchief, or rag, around her neck.

"Red is the blood in her veins that I can only imagine from this branch. They have an ascendant force; they want to take off, to escape, but are blocked by thick, rough fabric.

"I can whistle Nella's words for Ciaccio, her voice momentarily quelled by distance, while Dafne has locked her fists closed with her nails, her arms at her sides.

"She'll say: 'You're disgusting, and your father has nowhere else to hide. You're filth, a disgrace, and it's not enough for you to wear down the village, you've got to take this moron along—get thee to the brothel, you're nothing but a whore. It's going to end badly for you, when one day or another someone will equate your face with your backside and they'll find you beaten to death...'

"Then I see Ciaccio shaking, and his smile disappears.

"That smile, that seemed like an old scar that never left his face, was now hidden away somewhere toward the ground.

"Ciaccio is afraid, because to him Dafne is a star that fell at his side, and now, seeing that massive woman with that look of rage in her eyes just a few steps away, he knows that she is going to take her away from him.

"Quickly, he picks out a red ribbon, the nicest, and hands it to Dafne, looking at her wrist.

"'If you tie this on, nothing bad can happen to you,' he wants to tell her, but their eyes meet and nothing comes out of his mouth, barely a whimper.

"Dafne looks directly into Nella's big round face, and she even appears to overpower it. She passes it and stops near me, in this tangle of branches. I don't think she sees me, but when she responds to Nella, I know that along with the fog and Ciaccio, I have found a new friend.

"'If you don't get out of here, I'll smack you by twos until even becomes odd.'"

twenty-four

[what the flesh contains]

The flesh is a house, or a tool.

It's a rake, a spade, the grain of wood.

It's a kitchen, a chicken coop, a drawer, a clear beam of light that warms a window, or dust and runny ink, secret letters and spiderwebs, something creaking that can't be found.

Carnal love contains the idea of the species, fine embroidery for a trousseau, outdoor luncheons and vanished savings.

There's money, but also hatred, contempt, repugnance, and revenge.

There are the years in control and that warp you, and a parade of clothes, good soap, and white ash.

Nella has no sexual potency, nor has she ever, and now that Don Andreino has been transferred, she has lost her sentimental potency too, which was an act and an intoxication.

Dafne, however, with her immeasurable sexual power, sought out flesh not out of indecency, nor greed nor scandal, and certainly not for pleasure.

Nella turned around and left, reciting a rosary of threats under her breath. She couldn't have taken on a woman so much younger than her, who was agile, strong, and definitely crazy.

"We'll meet again," Nella thinks. "It doesn't end here, you spoiled whore."

Dafne follows her with her gaze, holding the red ribbon in her hand. When Nella disappears from view, Dafne places the ribbon in Ciaccio's hand, then leaves her hand in his.

The flesh is a horizon, or a clump of dirt.

The dead are there, in the flesh.

That's what Dafne was after.

twenty-five

[the jay and Dafne's victims]

"Seen from afar, we resembled a painting, one of those paintings that important museums in big cities reject because there are better ones of its genre, and no one needs a landscape by a drunken painter.

"But we weren't drunk, just still, and happy to be so.

"We were happy to be a bird, the village idiot, and the rebellious whore. Happy not to have money, but ribbons, the open air, a sense of wonder, and to be cursed or pitied by anyone. Happy to let time slip through our hands and wings without even noticing the sound it makes falling to the ground.

"No one liked those two, but I did, because since that day with the scene with Nella, they had taken to meeting often at the end of the field near the barn and I came along in my own way, above their heads, following them.

"They walked along with their backs to the houses, never turning around, and every once in a while, they held hands. It was always Dafne who reached for Ciaccio first, but in contrast to how she acted with the villagers, her movements were timid and hesitant, as if that contact were the manifestation of a long internal torment.

"They didn't speak much, and they didn't need to. A phrase here and there was enough; they understood each other intuitively.

"Ciaccio told her about Zuntura and me, without going back any further.

"But Dafne, like everyone else in town, knew the boy's origins, the story about the boat, Làinfondo, and all the rest.

"His entire account of me was contained in a gesture: lifting his arm and pointing at me. Dafne understood, and gave me a smile. She was a friend.

"Yes, words were left behind, superfluous, but not footsteps. We wandered off, sometimes, until we reached the bridge, where we were certain we wouldn't be followed. For often we were, though I didn't realize it at first. The followers kept a considerable distance, partly because they were afraid of Dafne's reaction, but mostly because the terrain, their terrain, didn't provide natural hiding places unless they went to the river where bushes and vegetation would have helped to conceal them, or near the bridge.

"Who were they? What did they want and what were they hoping to accomplish with their spying?

"They were Dafne's victims, jealous of the idiot. Sometimes Sergio came too, and once I saw Don Antonio's cassock. And then unfamiliar faces, people from elsewhere, probably men sent by Cosimo. Every one of them, whether from town or beyond, had some reason to follow Dafne and Ciaccio's innocuous walks. But not to the bridge, no—no one went as far as the bridge but the two of them.

twenty-six

[the bridge and its secret descendants]

"The reason is that the idiot and his companion aren't gullible unlike everyone else, that's why no one crosses me.

"They say that the man who had me built encountered a demon one night—not even an important one, because those ones are all in Rome—and confessed his fear of failing in the endeavor.

"He worried about the stones collapsing, the choice of a curved single span, the weight capacity, the safety of the men on the job, and above all the risk of human sacrifice, and apparently the creature responded that this was the minimum price, it even included a gracious discount in taking the souls of only two or three masons, considering the arrogance and vanity of building a bridge in the middle of nowhere for no other reason than to mortify the water below, where there was yet any kind of habitation, and this and no other was the exact reason the man was hanging on the words coming out of that demon's smoldering mouth, within reach of his writhing fiery tail.

"The man scowled, concentrated as he was on the task of joining the two hemispheres of his brain with a resolutionary bridge, precluding human sacrifice. But the hellish emissary, who frolicked in the thoughts of the weak like a child splashing in a pool of water, could see the torment in the mind of his interlocutor, and proposed a solution that would be acceptable to both parties.

"'Your construction shall be called Pontescuro,' he said, 'and so shall the village that will form around it. No bad will befall your workers. They will die of old age or stupidity, and you too will meet the same end. I will wait for the next generations. From them I will claim your debt, and in this way it will no longer involve you. What do you say? Does that seem reasonable? This is your deal with the devil..."

"The man thought for a moment, and then accepted with a smile.

"Given that he had no descendants, the only sacrifice he had to make was not to procreate. If he had no children of his own, the generation destined for the devil's clutches would mean nothing to him.

"That's my story, and that's how it has been passed down to this day.

"Grandmothers tell it and daughters pass it on; grandchildren memorize it to terrorize their younger siblings; even the dogs, who come nowhere near me, know it. And as long as this legend has existed, every generation has believed it, and believes itself the generation of the devil. Yet no one knows the entire story.

twenty-seven

[what is good and what is mad]

"You know what they say about this bridge?"

"No. Will you hold my hand again?"

"Yes. Well then?"

"Papa Zuntura doesn't want me to come here. But then he looks the other way if I do. He's good."

"Because he doesn't listen what to people say, that's what makes your father good. Mine doesn't listen other people either, but he's bad."

"Is the bridge good, Dafne?"

"It doesn't talk, and so it's good. Like your bird friend. Does he always follow you?"

"Yes. And he talks a lot. I know what he says. He talks a lot but he's good."

"Come on. Let's show them. Let's cross it."

"I don't know. Why do we need to show them? Who are we showing?"

"Whoever has no guts. Whoever can't see anything outside Pontescuro and is crushed inside it. Everyone."

"Then will they be mad at us?"

"They're already mad at us. Very mad. At me because they're hypocrites, they're fake and opportunistic, and they're poor. And I wave all that under their noses. All you have to do is walk toward them with your head held high and they're already offended, indignant."

"They're so stupid. Are they mad at me, too? Why?"

"Because you're free. The village idiot is always free."

"But they can walk over the bridge if they want to. I don't say not to. The bridge is free too."

"They prefer to stay away from it. The bridge is like my father: they want it to ask for magic. Occasionally they'll send a representative, like they do with my father, and ask for more money, more time, or for the river not to rise, not to act up and break the backs of the men loading the boats. But they're all broken already. I take care of the ones who are still upright."

"But you aren't bad. You hold my hand, and you like my red ribbons."

"If you like, when we get to the middle of the bridge, I'll give you a kiss."

"A kiss on the mouth?"

"On the mouth, yes, on the highest point on the bridge, that way we'll see the edge of the horizon. I think you'll like it."

"Do you know what Zuntura said to me once?"

"Let me think. That kisses can't be fixed?"

"No. That when you kiss a woman, it leads to Christmas."

twenty-eight

[a story about ancestors]

Sergio's forebear, builder of the dark bridge, didn't see many more Christmasies after his productive dalliance with the Roman peasant girl. He traveled between central Italy and the Po Valley, from one large estate to another, figuring out delays and agricultural problems, without realizing that it was his own life that had taken the path to unfixable ruin.

He was investigated for drowning a baby girl in a man-made rainwater canal whose construction he had showily endorsed, and from that point on his reputation dwindled to ruin, taking his entire body along.

The secret son, never baptized, was named Accorso by his grandparents, not so much after Buonaccorso or Buonaccorsi and the humanist legacy that would come with it, but more with the intention of branding him with the misfortune of his sudden lawless arrival. As soon as he could walk, he became a sneaky, vindictive swindler.

Of the two possible directions adulthood offered him to partially amend the fate he was born into, namely, the ability to spiritually connect with his fellow man or to rob said fellow man of his serenity, and ideally, money, he chose the latter, embellishing it with a display of charm.

As a result, he turned out nearly identical to his unknown father: he scattered the land with illegitimate children, many of whom were left in the foundling wheels in big cities.

One of them, calm and quiet as a clump of dirt dried out by a scorching sun, found the sweetness and good heart of a widow from Modena with a modest dowry. She hadn't had time to give her husband an heir, and in compensation, she showered this child from heaven with the most loving care and attention she was capable of giving.

Sergio's grandfather, whose name was Benvenuto, released the darker side of the bloodline by trading the opportunity to complete a formal education for learning how to rule over land, and especially those who fertilized the land with their own sweat.

Benvenuto achieved his goal and settled down in a small village not far from where he grew up, unaware of the significance of that little town, Pontescuro.

The power he accrued over the course of his life was slowly undermined and squandered by his youngest son, Adamo. He took on the literal meaning of his name, both son of the earth and man made of earth, weakening the ties his father had established with the political and administrative potentate of the area, namely the Casadio family.

When it came down to Adamo's only male offspring, all that was left of decades of hard work was the peasants' disdain, and the landlord, Cosimo Casadio's silent contempt.

Until one morning the thick ropes of decadent power transformed into a red ribbon around the neck of a beast. A vile female human animal.

But this cannot be said, because the female human animal that Sergio will find lifeless at the river's edge is the master's daughter.

twenty-nine

[Sergio figures out the trick of the dead]

"It's not the boat, he knows it's not the boat. The boat's further ahead, around the bend. Unless someone moved it. But no, that would be impossible. The wood's rotted, it's sunken into the ground. A water carcass wedded to the outgrowth of the earth. What strange thoughts. And what's the point of bringing her here? An idiotic effort, of no use. They try to spare themselves from toil whenever they can, my farm workers. But they can't. They're all work, and nothing else. They deserve nothing but work. And this isn't work. Maybe Ciaccio. But no, Ciaccio knows the interred boat was once his cradle. He stays away, he won't come here. And me? Why am I here now? What brought me to the river? Oh yes... now I remember. I wanted to figure out the trick, at least for a half an hour, an hour, first thing in the morning. How to live without responsibilities, that's the trick. Maybe smoke a cigar in peace. Be like Làinfondo, like Ciaccio. Or even Dafne, the rebel girl full of money. But no, let's leave her out of it, she could spit back that her work is the most serious, most difficult, most useful to the community. In any case, there is no trick, those strange people are simply empty inside. And I don't feel any lighter walking over uncultivated land, over land that's not work. Not at all."

"He threw me on the ground. He still hasn't realized I'm dead. He is confused, agitated. He doesn't know what's going on. He doesn't know who it was. He doesn't know why I'm here with him. He doesn't know why he did it. Did he do it? Who am I? Now he bends down, about to recognize me again. First a memory comes up. Can you taste it, Sergio, the bitter taste? That's nothing, there's more to come. Savor it. And wait, you can touch me. A few inches, a slight bend, and then finally you can touch me too. Like you always wanted. Then yes—your life will be bitter in the face of my death. Savor that memory."

"I remember how the windows were clouded with dirt and condensation, I had to wipe my entire forearm across it to see that it was you down the road. You advanced like a little sandstorm, a tornado of toxic air or contaminated water, and I, from my refuge, was hoping for an about-face at every step, a change of course, toward another house, another idea. I sensed your agitation, and the closest thing to an idea that you were capable of producing in that head of yours: revenge. Revenge and wariness. She'll be hiding a big rock in the pocket of her apron, a rusty broken scissor blade, or some kind of acid to throw in my face, I told myself. Everyone will see, but she doesn't care. The public humiliation I inflicted on her consumes her and gives her no peace, I told myself. If it wasn't for me, no one would have found out what type of communion crossed

Don Andreino and Nella's minds and bodies, I told myself, and in the meantime her figure loomed at the front door."

"And she offered you a deal instead. I know why she did it. You had prevented her from being with the only man willing to touch her, but I had rejected you without anyone's intervention. Nella knew it, and she knew how much my rejection burned you. She was prepared to bury the past and arrange a future with you that would at least bring with it the dignity of my death."

thirty

[the fog, the jay, the bridge, the river, the roach: an oratory of compassion]

"I wasn't the one to enter her lungs and burst them, nor to make her lose her way: what was she doing down there at night, maybe she wanted to wade across the river? Wash her defiled body? Was she coming from the barn with one of the many?"

"I don't know; when I rose up, she was already there, face down. For a moment her shape was still indistinct, for a moment I only saw a little red snake, nestled in a perfect circle, asleep. Then she emerged, in my center of vision. I must have been the first to discover her."

"Fog is bad for you. They'll say it again, but I, starting tomorrow, will come out thicker and darker in mourning."

"Dafne was sweet and I loved her, she was often a welcome accompaniment to my awakenings. Asleep or awake, that is the true distinction for these people. Not rich or poor, soft or work-worn hands, but whether one is asleep or awake. And here almost everyone is asleep. Asleep in the fields, hunched over, in their houses, at their stoves, with buckets in the stables, with cold water sprayed in their faces, at church in their Sunday best. Asleep. Dafne never slept and I'm sure she's not sleeping even now. She's dead, but not at rest."

"I was here already, I live here. I'm always here. I saw her first. She died twice, and they carried her on their shoulders to my feet. Her arms dangled in the air, like hands of a clock for the stars.

"Mine is a strange fate. To hover placidly and envelop Pontescuro, where by day nothing happens but by night newborns are abandoned, wine is gulped down while surroundings are taken in, tree trunks are embellished, birds are spoken to, the ground is doused in spit, and people are killed.

"You know what my dream is? That a heavy, cruel rain comes and doesn't stop falling until I swell up and flood.

"I would sweep away the houses, blessing them with water a little purer than what Don Antonio sprinkles in church. I would vindicate Dafne because I loved her too, but there's nothing I can do but flow by and look on."

"I could do something, but for what? Talking wouldn't help, they don't understand me. Spying, grasping their secret words the moment they're whispered—that's what I could do, but from afar, from the air.

"The houses are off limits to me, they would be cages, and their chimneys deadly traps. And then everyone would want me dead too because I'm a friend of Ciaccio's, and they can't kill Ciaccio.

"Zuntura would stop fixing things—in fact, he'd rig them, and bring ruin to their homes, and they know it. If there were a different space where I could find refuge, I'd wish for the sky to come crashing down on all of this. Caw, caw."

"Another space does exist and it's my home. Sometimes it's the ground, but more often it's underground. If there is shade and darkness, natural hiding places, it's better for me. I have a greater chance of survival. To go into people's homes, I need cracks, crevices, hollows, even wastewater can work well, if absolutely necessary. I have to rely on faulty vision, appeal to tired eyes, wine that dulls the senses and reflexes. They are minor things, happenstance defenses. Because if a kitchen light suddenly comes on in the night, I don't know who I'll find before me and I have to decide in a flash if I should curl up and stay still or anticipate a foot, a fist, a ladle that's already dented, any impromptu weapon, and start to run, run, run; run as fast as I can, without paying attention to the direction. Hundreds, thousands of my brothers and sisters have died this way. In houses the sunrise arrives at man's discretion. A finger on a switch and death comes on. I prefer soil, the pebbly sand of the river, little shrubs. There are risks there too, but better ones—natural, you could say. I'm part of nature too, in fact it always amazes me how much horror I invoke, the disgust, the killer instinct. Nota bene, I said Nature, I don't bother with God. God in a roach's mouth is something best left uncontemplated. People are already kneeling out of manners or opportunism, just imagine what they would do if I started in on theology. Forget it. Anyway, I was here when they brought her already dead body. I saw clearly the grimaces from effort and the beads of sweat on that murderous face. I know who did it. And it's best I go back in the ground. The true dangers of Pontescuro are above, in their faulty pursuit of cleanliness and order. I'm partial with the underground community. At least there no one kills anyone. In the charnel house of sustenance and survival where I live, no one would do what they did to Dafne."

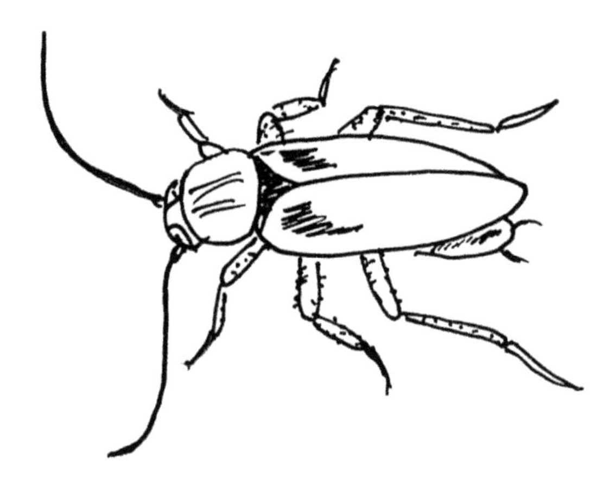

thirty-one

[an assembly of invalids]

Sergio passed through the center of town with a speed that seemed abnormal to everyone, accustomed as they were to seeing him with his legs firmly planted and arms akimbo like his beloved Romagnan idol, or if moving at all, walking slowly and pensively, with his chin pointed up to the sky, never as willful as he would have liked, occasionally lowering his gaze down to earth, and with a sneer of disgust, assessing the farmers' work.

Sergio was a fulcrum, a hinge, the pole of an enemy flag, even when carrying out his monotonous duties as overseer.

But that morning he crossed through town absent of these usual behaviors, a broken hinge, a pole toppled by wind, his face a tattered flag, crumpled and distorted.

He didn't look a living soul in the face, while in the fields, outside front doors, on dirt roads, men and women dropped whatever they were doing and saying, turning to him in astonishment, and as he headed toward Cosimo Casadio's castle, in fear.

In their collective memory, never had anyone, not even the steward, dared to knock on the master's door so early in the morning. Something terrible, unforgivable must have happened, an error that calls for harsh and immediate punishment.

Sergio shrunk as he ascended, and time could breath again, but now at a different pace.

In the limited clearing between Paolo di Ca' Bassa's and Giorgione's, crumbling and dusty houses that stood facing each other like two tired unarmed duelists, a throng of timorous onlookers gathered.

An assembly of invalids, demons secretly under their skin, arranged in a semicircle to be able to look into one another's eyes, their gazes binding them closely in a safety net. This is the impression they gave. Raggedy shades, wasting away, who now, under the sun now high in the emptiness, pitilessly highlighting their disturbance, were turned upside down: the humanity they had inherited churned in their guts and their private demons climbed up out of the darkness and spread across their features.

Gené felt like crying, but he didn't know why, and he moved quickly from one person to the next, gnawing on his nails, waiting for someone to tell him, "yes, cry, Gené, it's good for all of us." And his hands crept down there, because he had learned, on his own, in bed, how his breathing settled down afterwards, and his thoughts too, he could keep them under control, they became a thick silence inside a world of distant clouds and fluff, and once his hand fell back on the bare mattress he didn't care about anything anymore, and since he was afraid, now he had this enormous spiteful fear that shifted something in him, and it felt like everything that was Gené was slipping away and going somewhere else, but still inside him, and his hands were down his baggy underpants but before they could reach their destination Giorgione smacked him in the face, right there, where up until Sergio's appearance in town and his rush to the castle, there was Gené's cheek and now just a scrawny, sweaty question mark.

"You're a low-born, pig, freak, worse than Làinfondo, now even that bastard Sergio arouses you?"

Gené finally had reason to cry, and he was left aside to languish, like a fallen demon. There was no time to think about cheering him up, and no one wanted to anyway.

Paolo di Ca' Alta glared at Paolo di Ca' Bassa standing at the door to his house, a sorry sentinel, a miser, and thought, "the sun is so high, we need to figure out what's happening and defend ourselves, band together, and he doesn't even offer us a glass of wine, he has us dying of thirst; he's not even worthy of my name," and the other Paolo picked up on it, he could feel it on him, that silent resentment, that accusation with squinting eyes and hands in pockets, but what could he do, what did he expect, what did everyone want, him to empty his cellar one clean glass at a time, and maybe even some bread, as much as they wanted, while they were at it? No, he wasn't going to fall for that. "Is something terrible about to happen? And who cares, here everyone only thinks of themselves and I've done nothing wrong. I couldn't care less about Sergio and his rushing around."

Meanwhile, others had gathered in the clearing: Rico, Guglielmetto, Luciano, and a few young boys, but not many, most were with their fathers in the fields, summing up the only possible life in the only possible ledger.

Zuntura passed by, absorbed in turning a little iron and wood tool around in his hands, and stopped to listen. It was an old habit from his job as a handyman. To repair things, you have to listen to them first, get in tune with their problem to understand what's keeping them from working, that's the whole secret.

If he hadn't realized that God can't be fixed when he was young, he could have been the local priest.

However, besides his tools, he still had people, and that unplanned gathering was good practice. He stopped to listen, determined not to speak, not even if asked.

In broken sentences, insults, accusations, raised voices, and gestures, the event was reconstructed. Sergio had passed through town with an upset look on his face, and headed for the castle. He hadn't said a word, and he hadn't looked at anyone. That was it, nothing more.

The object he had in his hand made a loud click, tlak, and at that moment Zuntura realized that actually, there was more.

There was the fact that his son was missing.

There was the fact that Nella was missing.

thirty-two

[secret woods and rings around the rosie]

Nella had gone to see Don Antonio at the rectory.

She wanted to make her confession, but not in the traditional way, kneeling in a corner of the church.

She wanted to talk.

The priest was amazed to see her there, on a day so far from mass and at an hour when no one since his arrival in Pontescuro had ever shown up asking for advice, consolation, or dispensation from the sins of their soul.

He invited her to have a seat on a bench, and he sat down on a wooden chair shielded by a small table, because he was aware that that woman, in that place, was something much worse than a common sinner. He folded his hands, rested his elbows on an open missal, and waited.

Dafne had taught Ciaccio ring around the rosie, how fast to go to keep your head from spinning, and even a little rhyme to sing while they spun around with their arms open wide.

Together they had discovered an uncultivated patch of land far from the river and the houses a fifteen-minute walk from the bridge, and that morning the boy had woken up earlier than usual to get there because Dafne had suggested they meet there, telling him that ring around the rosie was much more fun surrounded by wildflowers.

He had dressed in a hurry, and without stopping to greet Zuntura, he had left. She had perhaps forgotten or had some business to attend to in the barn, he had no way of knowing; nevertheless, she hadn't come. Ciaccio was sad, but in his own way, still with a smile on his lips. The world couldn't be any better as long as the ribbons in his box didn't run out. And Zuntura was an attentive father.

For the first time since she had begun flying around him, the jay perched on his shoulder. She didn't even fly away when Ciaccio opened his arms, and singing softly, made the earth around him spin.

Cosimo Casadio resisted the temptation to throw Sergio out before showing him to his sitting room. Naturally, it wouldn't have been his style, but so early in the morning proper manners with his subordinates were slow to manifest, and that man, whom he didn't like and never had, knew his stuff, which included the ability to recognize a propitious or adverse moment, and thus had decided to hear him out.

Sergio tried to tame his jagged breath, and then began to talk about Dafne.

The ability to listen and judge well was evident and placid in Don Antonio.

His evangelical mission was never completed; rather, he thought of it as an unplanned journey, and the invisible yet weighty baggage he brought along were the robes of doubt, weakness, and identification with evil, which he didn't consider as such, because as a learned man he knew that clear-cut distinctions work for land ownership but not for lending the soul.

He was mulling all this over now with Nella, reviewing it as if to reinforce it, because this woman was uniquely capable of unnerving him. He knew exactly what she intended, and that was to convince him that she was a good woman who had been a victim of misfortune. But the target of that act of persuasion remained impenetrable, and highly irritating the method she used and that entailed the salvation of her own person, burying everyone else in detail with examples of daily insignificances and, at her suggestion, very serious stains hidden in some mysterious place.

Despite being up on all the relationships between the individual inhabitants of Pontescuro, and in the present case, Nella's opinions of this person or that, and they of her, Don Antonio, in an exercise of abstraction, observed from above this woman's urgency to obtain social absolution, among the community more than in the church, and the only explanation that came to his however murky and addled mind, was that something strange was about to happen in the village.

So Don Antonio, so as not to offend her, asked her very cautiously, using elegant circumlocutions, if she knew of some strange event that was going on, had just happened, or was about to occur.

The woman, in response, declared that it had gotten very late and that she had to go.

It was ten in the morning.

Ciaccio, craning his neck, talked with the jay for a long time. He discovered an eloquence in himself he didn't know he had, and above all, that with her it was an easy game because, caw caw, not only did she understand him, she helped him formulate his haziest thoughts. She drew them out with her lively, tiny eyes, encouraging him with the delicate flutter of her wings. Ciaccio felt at home. He opened up his heart to her and the words poured out, even the ones he didn't know very well, like Worry and Pain.

Cosimo had Sergio take him to the place where the body had been found, but not before making a series of telephone calls to people who, at his word, would rush over to Pontescuro. Someone to compile the documents, someone to arrange for burial, and someone to bring the perpetrator of the misdeed to justice.

Sergio, his head down, agreed, prepared to do whatever his master asked of him. He set off ahead. He made way for a father without tears, his face stony, his back straight, and for a moment, he was afraid.

thirty-three

[an anomalous calm]

But he came back to himself at the thought of Dafne's necklace. That pendant hanging around her milky neck was reassurance for him and for all of his fellow villagers. All except one, obviously.

They passed right in front of him—Sergio had chosen the road along the houses and not the one through the fields so as to be seen side-by-side with the master in serious conversation—and just when the steward lengthened his stride and nudged Cosimo's elbow as if to walk arm-in-arm, Cosimo stopped abruptly in front of Ca' Bassa's house, turned to the human stain and ordered him to follow him.

"You wanted my daughter's body?" he said. "Now come and get it."

No one dared reply.

The questions stuck in their throats, where the sins of each burned aflame. They kept their mouths shut, but if it were possible to listen inside, one could have heard the secrets, the pettiness, and unspoken pacts they'd all made, with themselves or perhaps with an accomplice, crackling as they tried to rise up and escape their bodies to vanish into the air.

But all that which had been done could have filled a depository heavier than a ship full of cargo, was more cavernous than a granary after a threshing, and with that invisible freight, the procession set off, supplemented by the addition of Nella, who had suddenly appeared near the church.

In Rome, it was easy to decide which functionary should be sent to Pontescuro.

In the offices, they leafed through archives, opened drawers and files, and then someone remembered the name of the town, the young landowner, the river transports, and the farm worker strikes quelled with a few yawns and pats on the back, and came to the appropriate conclusion.

"The problem with these petty landowners is they think the world revolves around them, but in reality the more the world forgets about them the better everything works."

This philosopher, also head of the judicial police, glad to have imparted a lesson on proper tactical and psychological strategy to whomever was lingering in the room at that moment, concluded his brief statement with an authoritative command: "Get Romanelli."

Don Antonio estimated the time it would take to avoid Nella anywhere outside or nearby the church, and then with his prayer book under his arm, decisively emerged from the rectory.

Where he would have expected the usual serenity of the early workday, he was instead met with an anomalous calm, emptied out, as though during his chat with the woman his church had been transported to an exotic desert.

He stared up toward the sun for a second, squinted, and looked around. The heat showed him a familiar panorama.

They must be somewhere, he thought, and he set off toward the fields to look for Ciaccio. He, at least, shouldn't be too hard to find.

But he was wrong. Instead he found Zuntura, stock still in the middle of the field like a scarecrow. He was calling his son's name and scanning the tree branches in desperation.

And thus the priest realized the situation.

He placed a hand on the man's shoulder and gently turned him around.

"Let's go to the river," he said. "You'll see that Ciaccio will turn up. He can't be too far."

thirty-four

[wax figures]

Once a clergical robe appeared, the scene of the crime took on the semblance of a timeless and ritualistic space.

A miasma of earthy sacrality mixed with sweat and anger was in the air, penetrating far beyond the discovery site of that still-young corpse. And despite not yet having received a report, Cosimo's trusted men were surely already on their way. Dafne appeared disheveled with her eyes closed, and almost all of the men crowded around her had imagined her at least once in that exact position, something that now became a sort of mirage in their thoughts, a picture card from so many dreams and restless nights, by some witchcraft cast into a no man's land without beds or hay.

One glance was enough for Don Antonio to realize he was looking at the whirlpool that had sucked up all the noise, and that strange silence he had sensed just minutes before in the street was only the long wave of an interment, of breath collectively held, while Cosimo Casadio's voice snaked through the interstices of that trance, that terror.

They were wax figures, standing there motionless, in a circle forming a funeral wreath around Dafne's lifeless body.

Sergio finally found the courage to interrupt Cosimo's vague accusations.

It was the red ribbon that gave him the idea and put the fire back in his eyes.

It was so obvious, everyone saw it: Ciaccio had disappeared, but had left his signature.

Hunt him down and put him to justice, that's what they needed to do together, Sergio shouted, while Nella nodded.

Strangle him in front of her father, cut off his head and take it to the castle. The proper offering for an inauspicious season.

But Cosimo Casadio interrupted his outcries, turning to Don Antonio and ordering his daughter's body be taken to the church.

The legal authorities, despite not tarrying and leaving promptly, as he was a person of importance, wouldn't be able to arrive until late afternoon, if not evening or after dark, in which case it was just as well to remove his daughter from that place.

Everyone to church, the master thundered. And no one is to leave until further notice. Until order is restored.

Don Antonio said nothing but prayed silently for each of them. He said their names in his mind one by one, ending with the souls he considered the most innocent and unblemished

Dafne.

Ciaccio.

thirty-five

[Inspector Eugenio Romanelli shifts the center of gravity]

It certainly couldn't be said that Eugenio Romanelli moved apace with the years.

1922 brought Italy militias and Fascist paramilitary squads, discipline polished with buckets of castor oil and elbow grease to preserve national security, vigorous enthusiasm, and new slogans.

There was a widespread sense of institutionalized violence and a changing of the guard.

Il Duce even stated as much, in his booming voice: "Men must be led; they're not capable of getting anywhere on their own!"

Inspector Romanelli, on the other hand, didn't entertain a single doubt about which direction he ought to take in his life: retirement, rest, and silence.

He was born in 1861 in Romano Canavese, a little town about 50 kilometers from Torino, which shared with the capital of the Kingdom of Italy the scepter of an elegant peace; it shook it a little, seeking admiration from the young nation, yes, but with discretion and from a considerable distance.

And if the inhabitants of a place are anything like the place they inhabit, it would be hard to find a better example than Romanelli: an only child from a poor family, a solitary and pensive child, a curious and composed adolescent,

the young Eugenio developed an uncommon analytic ability that didn't escape his parents, who, making a considerable financial sacrifice, sent him to study in the big city to become somebody important, redeeming himself and them. At least that's what they had hoped.

Eugenio did what he could to please them, but he couldn't ignore his natural inclination to put himself aside to help others get ahead.

He didn't consider his life worthy of grand attentions, but something without victimization or dramatic poses: a simple, objective, self-evident truth. Or Lapalissian, as he had learned from his fellow students.

Being a disciple of La Palice endowed him with a special quality, which was to play a decisive role in his life: invisibility. Eugenio Romanelli went unnoticed, unseen, undetected.

In the daylit cafés, between stucco walls and inlaid wooden tables, or on the street in the evening, when people return home and the urban murmur dissipates and dies down, or in a lecture hall, shoulder to shoulder with his classmates—no matter the circumstance, Eugenio Romanelli was essentially absent.

The personal and social consequences of this became evident soon enough. He never found a wife to stand at his side, and once he was freed of his sense of obligation by the premature death of both parents, he redirected his studies to a very different institution, a place where invisibility took you straight to the top: the police.

Forty-one years and a long series of transfers later—Turin to Milan, to Rome, to Naples, and then to the most remote provinces of central Italy and finally back to Rome—at his superior's order ("get Romanelli"), called out indistinctly in the law enforcement offices, the sixty-two-year-old Eugenio, was already right there in the room.

He was sitting in a corner under the window, examining his hands and shifting a satisfied gaze at his well-manicured nails to a perplexed view on the outside world, specifically consisting of an empty Roman courtyard, in the middle of which his 1912 Itala was parked, in decidedly worse shape than his fingernails.

This action, or rather, pendulous inaction, namely the observation of two rather distinct manifestations of reality, back and forth, back and forth, to the point of unmasking their affinities, had given him some unexpected yet often useful results over the course of Romanelli's long career.

His colleagues, seeing his effectiveness, had even stopped mocking him, and he, patient and completely unfazed, at each case closed would explain from the beginning each individual step that led him to the culprit; perhaps the color of a shirt, or as was the case in his years of rural investigations, the eye of a surviving cow.

In the good old days, his colleagues and superiors gathered around him, and he fielded all their numerous questions.

His method wasn't complicated, he would reply, flattered and patient; it was a matter of giving credit to the banal and the ordinary, and concentrating on the margins, the gray areas—ultimately, peering into the impasses of the investigation. The dead spots, he would say, are never actually dead, just as we often fail to see what is right in front of us.

It was simple to comprehend, not so easy to apply, because one could learn the method, but not the speculative sensibility.

Those happy years lasted quite some time, and as a man fixated on tiny details, he didn't notice just how quickly they were passing by.

He secured an advance, which was considered more like a tactical investment, and he purchased an automobile—an Itala with a red body and rims, with the spare tire on the passenger side door like a life preserver.

He named it Eugenia and treated it like the wife he never had, and with it, up and down all over town, he really did save some people by getting dozens of delinquents, even a few murderers, thrown in jail.

When his golden years lost their luster, his assignments diminished and the mockery towards him grew, albeit with a certain deference, given his professional seniority.

That morning, Eugenio Romanelli's contemplative disposition was trained on the point of melancholy equidistance where his existence idled—three months since his last case, three months to retirement—when he was called upon.

There was a gentleman from a small town to the North whose daughter had been murdered.

He was a widower, his first three sons had run off years ago, and he'd thrown a fit on the telephone, flaunting high-level acquaintances and demanding a full investigative commission.

Did Romanelli really want to dust off his old motorcar and head off to see what he could do?

Eugenio Romanelli rose from his chair, nodding.

His melancholy's center of gravity shifted.

thirty-six

[behind the temple door]

In theory it wasn't that different from mass, Don Antonio thought, leaning against the altar. A good mass, well-attended.

The church is the place of the community assembled under the benevolent gaze of the crucified Christ, he thought, and one speaks softly in the presence of the savior on the cross, and so they did now.

It was a trick so as not to give in to the whispers, which were mounting nonetheless as the hours passed. Much like his fear.

"Say something, are you the priest or aren't you? No, not a sermon, it's too late for that now. Just calm them down. Talk about calm and peace," Don Antonio thought. "About future peace. Peace where there is no future. The peace that everyone will come to, sooner or later."

No, it's not a mass, it's a funeral service, a last goodbye, Don Antonio thought, and he lowered his eyes onto Dafne's body there before him, laid out as best they could on some planks someone brought in from outside.

In theory it wasn't so different from a wake, Don Antonio thought, sweat streaming down his back under his black cassock.

What was missing, was a casket, flowers on top. There was only the body, laid out unadorned, Cosimo's grim expression, and the whispers.

No one dared move, no one would open the temple door, no one.

"I should pray out loud," Don Antonio thought. "Requiem aeternam, Gloria Patri, Pater Noster, Salve Regina, an Ave, maybe Veni Creator Spiritus. I have to drown out the whispering, because I'm starting to catch some of what they're saying, and I don't like it."

Drive far away our wily Foe, and Thine abiding peace bestow; if Thou be our protecting Guide, no evil can our steps betide.

"Pontescuro is cursed, and we all of us will pay."

The Fount of life, the Fire of love, the soul's Anointing from above.

"She asked for it, she went looking for it, we're innocent."

Come, Holy Ghost, Creator blest, Vouchsafe within our souls to rest.

"The Master will push us, work us to death, break our backs."

Fill the hearts which Thou hast made.

"Cursed be the day that baby appeared at the river."

Thy light to every thought impart and shed Thy love in every heart.

"Yes, it's his fault. He brought us misfortune. Why hasn't he been found yet?"

Make Thou to us the Father known; teach us the eternal Son to own.

"The misfortune was there before he was. The entire village was built on misfortune."

Amen.

thirty-seven

[over the hill]

"Amen," said Eugenio Romanelli, bent over the Itala's smoking engine. At least the trip was almost over. There was one last hill to cross, beyond which, if his maps weren't wrong, he would run smack into the township of Pontescuro.

Moreover, walking was an activity that stimulated the processing of thoughts; he would take advantage of this, perhaps following along the river, which, if his maps weren't wrong, was located on the slope of the hill, just past the castle, a little neglected in truth, as he saw now through his binoculars, closing Eugenia's hood with an extra pat; after all, a good wife all these years.

Despite his sixty-two years and retirement imminent on paper but unofficially already in effect after many months of inactivity—this, he knew, would be his last, unanticipated case— Romanelli had remained slim and muscular, in stark contrast with the physical tendencies of any post-war period that impose fat or at least a little pudge as evidence of newfound health and prosperity. In the office, one of his oft-repeated maxims, directed at his heftier colleagues, said: “eating may shape the belly, but it doesn’t sharpen the intellect.”

Having kept faith in his body now proved especially useful, and he set off at a swift pace.

Over the hill, just as it started to slope down, copious evidence for his investigation began to appear.

He took a little yellow notebook and a pencil out of his jacket pocket and, still walking, started to write.

thirty-eight

[three signals for the dark]

A procession of cockroaches in an anomalous and long orderly line was descending into the valley, flanked by a second, fainter line, blurry and teeming at about a meter's distance. Closer examination revealed that it was composed of ants of various sizes and pine processionaries, of dirty-white worms and fat slugs, earthworms, millipedes, and other creatures with tiny round shells.

Romanelli took notes.

The boats were lined up on the river, keel to bow, as though they were stuck or waiting for permission to set sail. They looked like enormous insects, bellies up, their legs the cargo tied down and piled in columns.

Romanelli took notes.

Disoriented flocks flew low in frenzied formations, with different yet indistinguishable species, swooping fast toward the highest point of the village, the bell tower of Pontescuro.

The landscape lay open like a fan, but the air was stifling.

Eugenio Romanelli, still taking notes, arrived at the foot of the village with its depleted supplies, its flying arrows overhead.

"They sent me inside a postcard. An old postcard from a vintage shop.

"I'm entering the basement of a warehouse, a back-alley market of broken, lost, stolen things, the fetor of a dark stairwell, and all by the light of day, which is not enough.

"Here the daylight is not enough, my dear Eugenio. What you're seeing is reality's underbelly. They've found a way to turn everything on its back. A dead girl? Here, the case of the strangled girl will be the easiest thing to unravel."

He closed the notebook and headed straight for the bell tower.

thirty-nine

[blood for blood]

The space of the presbytery represents the head of Christ: the transept represents the arms, the altar represents the heart, and the aisle represents the body.

The first jay crashed into the wall near the little aisle, making a miniature boom that they attempted to interpret as the portent of a hailstorm. But it wasn't the season or even the place, and they knew it.

"A single noise matters little. Fear, speculation, they don't really help understand what works and what doesn't, here we are all afraid," Zuntura thought, meanwhile keeping an eye on the pews.

Everyone had turned toward the noise, while a second jay slammed violently into the front door behind the worshippers, and a third almost simultaneously hit the eastern cornice.

On the roof over the altar, where Don Antonio had increased the volume of his prayers to the point of shouting, a fifth, sixth, and seventh jay splattered the roof with feathers and broken wings, while a thicker, bigger flock was breaking apart just a little further up, in perfect vertical alignment with Dafne's face below.

They were just the vanguard.

The suicide bombing escalated, and it was likely some of the people assembled imagined that a giant hand had tapped its funders to test the miserable resistance of that holy place and was now trying to crush it to the ground.

Fear is a fickle mother. She can give birth to kindness and solidarity or hostility and accusations.

Don Antonio's voice was drowned out by a brood of new arrivals, each one of them well equipped to inflict injury, and possibly butcher.

The people were ready to exchange blood for blood, as in the ritual of sacrifice, with the dead woman in front of them and the great door behind them, slowly opening.

Eugenio Romanelli entered an arena of consecrated carnage born of fear and barely restrained by it.

forty

[the procession]

"My brothers and the creatures like me from the underground reached the river and followed its path with certainty. They knew the destination.

"Many of them, hundreds, thousands, had never been here."

Even so there was no hesitation in those soft padding steps, as if a center of operations located far beyond the tip of their antennas transmitted with resounding precision the coordinates of a destination now half-buried, hidden in the vegetation, inert to the rest of the world but of fundamental importance.

That code, which the birds could hear too, was instructions for the conclusion.

They would go to the rotting boat.

They would go to Ciaccio's cradle.

forty-one

[prison on credit]

The first impression was clear—a bunch of lunatics. They seemed like lunatics to him.

They were barely more composed—their eyes basically in their sockets and their hair more or less neat, compared to the example portraits found in his office in Rome, that his boss, a Cesare Lombroso fanatic, had imposed on his team with the enthusiasm of a Futurist exhibition curator.

Romanelli found Lombroso to be rather hard to swallow and had deemed his theories of physiognomy and phrenology outlandish assertions lacking scientific accuracy, imbecilic, even demented, fabrications.

Yet now his twentieth-century enlightenment was scrunched up in a corner of his mind, mortified and suffering, and it only took two or three steps into the church to redirect his firmest convictions toward no man's land, or rather, madman's land.

He crossed this black sabbath heading toward the priest, whom he had identified from the back of the church with the relief of a lost sea captain spotting the bright flash of a lighthouse.

But before such a rational approach, he had to encounter the dead.

He went around her, lost in thought.

She was a girl who went far beyond her beautiful appearance; the fixity of the end had yet to set in, or perhaps it had enhanced her, bringing a certain serene grace to her features in such a way that her face seemed like the box of the universe containing the treasure of all forgiveness.

Those too, Eugenio noted, weren't thoughts that could come from him. They weren't rational. But he couldn't put them out of his mind.

In the past he had dealt with obsessives, which his colleagues also called possessed, deep down just other poor, unhappy people, and he knew what it took to untether a stubborn thought: if its opposition is ineffective, the thought should be left to go on to its conclusion, observed neutrally as though it had nothing to do with you. The obsessive thought, unsatisfied, will leave you on its own.

Obsessions live and feed on opposition, they wallow in guilt, in ancestral fears, in inner struggle, and only by emptying these stores will we starve them enough to drive them out.

Who knows if this unfortunate girl, thought Romanelli, abandoning his circumnavigation of the remains and heading right to Don Antonio with his hand extended, had offered her fellow villagers the same subdued elegance in life.

Looking into all their eyes, I would swear the opposite.

The priest, coming in closer and speaking softly, recounted what he knew: the discovery of the body at the river and everything else.

Cosimo, unable to tolerate being excluded from a dialogue between spiritual and temporal power that he himself had requested, with the latter, judging by instinct, a bit subpar, went over to join the two, and integrated the information, telling Romanelli, with no scruples or shame, that this girl was his daughter, and just who this daughter was the daughter of, and what the girl had been doing in town, and how everyone hated her, even those who had had the chance to love her, and for that reason identifying the killer would be no easy task.

The lunatics, in the meantime, sat motionless in the pews, but Cosimo's conclusion was heard in the front rows, prompting contributions from Nella and Sergio who, having overcome their sense of deference to the master, fattened the policeman's notebook with a few other elements relevant to the investigation, so they thought—an aggressive and conclusive accusatory act, thought Romanelli.

"I don't like quick conclusions," Romanelli thought. "And where is this Ciaccio, anyway? Why isn't he here? What was his relationship to the victim?"

"Hold on, please. Let's calm down and start over. Absence does not automatically signify guilt. If that were the case, there would be an endless merry-go-round on which everybody would sooner or later be accused of murdering someone else."

"If all unsolved crimes followed such a rule," he continued with a smile restrained by circumstance, "life would be prison on credit, a waiting room to conviction. And I would have no reason to exist," he concluded.

From the pulpit, addressing the entire church, he ordered them all to return to their homes or to work. He would question them, one by one. And keep calm.

He would be in the rectory, which Don Antonio had kindly made available to him as an office.

The lunatics' only response was loud and clear: find the boy and take him away. Far away from there, behind bars, in the big city, to another place, another world.

Because Ciaccio was the one who had murdered Dafne.

forty-two

[savior colony]

"I found myself alone, and stopped crawling. My brothers and sisters will catch up to me. Maybe we'll submerge ourselves in the river, maybe we'll go away. We'll search for new land. I haven't decided yet. But I have to hurry. My life cycle is ten weeks. And I don't intend to lay eggs. Not this time. Not worth it. I got a good look at Sergio, his strained expression and pools of sweat. The body slid from his shoulders, dangling, and wouldn't keep still. He wanted to enter that body, hurt it, inseminate it with hate, with his dripping appendage. And he was about to. It was when he could no longer manage the slippage that in a fit of rage, instead of allowing her to slide from his shoulders, he lifted her in the air and threw her to the ground with all his might.

"He was unbuttoning his filthy, disgusting pants when my colony emerged from all four corners of the dark and surrounded him.

"They died under the soles of his shoes, one by one, all of them.

"All except me."

forty-three

[misery isn't clean]

Pontescuro's secrets cracked open like overheated eggs in that rectory, but Romanelli felt useless.

We've been working the land for generations, they told him, and what did he think land was? An elegant table set with fine silverware and glasses clear as air? Where you make yourself comfortable all dressed up and clean cut like a true gentleman, and can gorge yourself dish by dish without a spot on your cuffs or chin, served by perfumed waitresses and a host as radiant as the sun? Sorry, Inspector, but no. That's not how it works. You came to our table, scrutinized our plates, and didn't try a thing, just questioned us. What is this recipe, what ingredients did you use there, is our wine aged in oak—and most importantly, does the kitchen meet the standards for hygiene. And we answered. But you didn't like our answers. What did you expect? Here we get by however we can. The soil here is tainted, if you must know—in fact, it's disgusting underneath, and the master is dirty too. Even the fruit we manage to extract from this land isn't clean, because as soon as we gather it they take it away, paying us a pittance, the usual scrap keeping us in misery, the same poverty that grips us up from the day we're born and follows us to the grave. And you know, Inspector, poverty isn't clean, and we live in it, and living in it we get dirty, nothing unusual about that. Yes, we're dirty and we make do as we are. Dafne offended us, all of us. She offended our mothers, our wives, our future women that are our poor daughters, daughters of poverty, because she flaunted her loveliness, she looked upon our women's misery and spat on it with her beauty. And she offended our men, the misery of our boys bent over in the fields, children with wrinkles, old people with shot knees, and she did it with seduction. She insulted us with seduction. And we walked right into it, like nasty insects lured by poison bait, like rats, we were ensnared by that seduction. But we are not destined for beauty. It's not our destiny, many of us don't even know the meaning of words like possibility, fulfillment, love—they're traps, trying to pursue those things, circling around them, you die, a slow death—just like poison. You see, Inspector, we take care of things on our own, we stick to our own, we resolve matters our own way, and anyone who has other ideas, those who are in thrall to all the beauty that has nothing to do with us, whether a property of man or of nature itself, we render it powerless, we neutralize it, we push it to the margins of our land, whether it's a mute drunk, a proponent of liberty, an ignorant poet, a dreamer. But a girl, even a provocative girl, for us remains untouchable, believe it; sure, we fed on her provocation, but we never would have killed her because we understand the vendetta of beauty, we know it by instinct, whether a property of man or of nature itself. So why are you here? Dreams kill dreams, and there's nothing more to it. It is most certainly not us—the excluded, the condemned—who killed the daughter of Cosimo Casadio. It couldn't have been anyone but a dreamer.

As you say in the law, convict the boy by default and go home. You can leave finding him to us. We, spiteful hoarders of misery, who offer sex to priests, drink ourselves into a stupor, don't know joy, we who wield useless tools, who live in shacks and in decrepit houses—we, in fact, are the innocent ones.

forty-four

[putting the witnesses to sleep]

The words used by the interrogated in the rectory, however, were quite different. The articulation, the particular collective sense, the meaning behind the moods and fears, the stuttering and swearing, was carefully reconstructed in the dead of night, the last, by Eugenio Romanelli.

He filled his notebook to the end, then reread it, sitting at the small mirror hung in the corner next to the bed for ablutions in the room that Don Antonio had provided for him.

Finally, he closed it up and burned it, using an entire box of matches.

The ideal solution, at that point.

There was his retirement around the corner. The last stretch was long, of course, before he would get there, but Eugenio knew perfectly well that the moment he stepped on Eugenia's footboard (in the meantime Furàza had gotten her up and running), Pontescuro would disappear, and not just into the horizon and out of his mind, but from the entire panorama of events. Even in the police archives, in Rome, his dossier would be forgotten, never moved from the drawer where it would be put away.

In time, everything happens unbeknownst to the witnesses. That's what time does: put the witnesses to rest.

Even men like him, accustomed to reading reports, who live on evidence the way other people survive on air, fall asleep sooner or later. And time gets its revenge. On the unsuspecting and aware alike. It gets its revenge on everyone.

Pontescuro was the world that formed after the end of every known world. And Romanelli, packing up his belongings in the open suitcase on the bed, now knew how one lives after everything has ended. He knew in detail, including names and nicknames.

Burning that notebook was an act of pure justice.

There was a small window in the rectory that faced the back of the church, toward the open fields. Who knows how that little domestic bonfire looked from the outside.

So Romanelli wondered, then smiled bitterly. Perhaps he was thinking of the wife he never had. Then yes, instead of being in the place where the people who live in the world after the world ends go to pray with his suitcase gaping open like the mouth in the middle of his disdainful face, he and his wife could have admired the soothing lights of the neighbors' windows, where other couples, embraced like them behind the glass, would be waving hello, smiling imperceptibly in the dark.

Instead, the darkness out there now seemed like an entity of evil, the very skin of a giant polymorphous creature, its chest expanding as it wheezed and breathed in vital sustenance, what little remained, the survivors, even if far away and indistinguishable: stars, clouds, winged and earthly creatures, while those on the ground, in the underground, who continued their laborious digging in the dirt and damp because they had yet to realize that the world had ended.

Before closing up his suitcase Eugenio Romanelli wrote a brief report, using the formulas and phrases protocol demanded. He felt conflicted with the pangs of conscience, but wrote it all the same.

He wrote the details of the investigation and faithfully reported the statements of the many witnesses.

He wrote that Dafne Casadio's murderer was a poor half-wit without a name, a foundling whom everyone called Ciaccio because he cawed like a bird.

He wrote that the victim indiscriminately gave her body to the men in the village and that, in all probability, she had denied the same favor to the aforementioned Ciaccio and he took his revenge. Considering the subject's inability to understand, in other words, he was unable to mitigate the force of his disappointment, his anger, and on a lethal impulse, most likely considered by him to be an act of love, he tightened one of his red ribbons around the girl's neck, the ones everyone knew that the murderer used to senselessly decorate the trees in the area.

He is the material executor of an abstract collective mandate, Romanelli wanted to add, but he kept this sentence to himself. His superiors could only understand one world at a time.

He closed the suitcase and prepared to leave.

forty-five

[a spot in the fog]

"You know fog? They say it's bad for people.

"Fog has always been very important in these parts. However, it is one of those intangible events that determines who you are merely by observing it from one point or another or being inside of it. It determines why you have your name, and what the house you sleep in is like, and on what bed, if it is indeed a bed.

"But in truth, I'm not so harsh. In fact, to prove it, I'll show you something.

"He's become a speck in the incipient emptiness, can you see? Hurry up, because he's about to disappear. After all, his was a borrowed bed and going back to the shack to collect all his cords and ribbons would have been too far a walk, and anyway it had been Dafne who taught him that you should never go back, that it's wiser to keep moving forward.

"She explained to him what wisdom is, and laughing softly, she told him that thing that had made him blush without even noticing.

"She told him he'd been born that way, wise, what did she need to explain it for.

"All the things he'd learned from Dafne! Love, certainly, which now he knew how to identify. That had been a difficult apprenticeship, because it wasn't a single feeling, it was many things at once, and keeping them all together pushed you to the limits of human possibility. Now he could truly say he loved Zuntura, the trees, the jay and her sisters, the fields, the flowers, and his girlfriend, Dafne. Because Dafne had been his girlfriend, she had told him so, in a whisper.

"When I get away from here, you can tell everyone that I only had one boyfriend in Pontescuro, and that was you."

"How exciting that had been! It was a secret that bounced around inside of him, like ring around the rosie, but it made Ciaccio shiver, too, because he didn't want Dafne to go away anywhere.

"Fear of abandonment was stronger than the discovery of having a sweetheart. But then she took him by the hand and his anguish dissipated. And there were so many other walks, eventually he forgot all about it.

"Until that day.

"That day Dafne didn't come. They had agreed to meet at the bridge, just as they had done for some time. She would appear smiling, scurrying up to him. Then he would see the jay appear somewhere high in the sky, and join them with a whistle.

"That day his feathered love swooped down from behind and landed on his shoulder without a sound.

"The sky is a welcoming mystery: every so often a guest will cross it, a lone flyer or flock, an atmospheric mass.

“A jay’s path, so vast in proportion to its dimensions, to transport a bit of straw, a twig, natural fibers, back and forth, to build a nest, a landing, safety, support, rest, tranquil sleep, or to provide silence.

“The jay provided silence that day, and for Ciaccio, who didn’t know what to do, his feet provided the answer. He discovered that where the fields he knew ended, others began, not so different from the ones before and yet new, mysterious, surprising.

“‘If Dafne doesn’t find me, I’ll find her,’ he said to himself, and set off on his journey.”

forty-six

[Ciaccio on his journey]

Ciaccio's mind wandered as he walked, because it was nice to get deep into thought as it was into the unfamiliar fields.

He thought about the world's particularities, his days, his life. The idea that he could get away from here, from Pontescuro. That his life wasn't a limit, but rather an infinite line.

There's no preservation, possession, order to feelings, security. Stick out your neck, Ciaccio, not for the executioner but for passion. The trees are greener and clearer behind the shade, and you know you're broken, and that's your beauty.

You're Ciaccio, walking, keeping his head high, and expanding his horizon. The earth, having held you in its womb and witnessed barbarities you have no idea of, hums under your feet.

You know what that vibration is? It's a memory, it's Ciaccio on his journey, a memory that became conscious, a repository for what you've lost, for what you'll never have again.

But your memory is also a resonance, and rest assured, it will be picked up by someone, years, decades in the future, when the speck that you're becoming will have dispersed.

forty-seven

[beyond Pontescuro]

The jay perched on Ciaccio's shoulder and brushed his cheek with her beak. It was a kiss.

She was coming from the scene of the crime. She had seen and heard and was very sad, but didn't want to tell the boy.

She had seen Dafne overturned, the red ribbon around her neck. She had seen the cold eyes of Dafne's father and the grimaces, the furrowed looks, the hidden hands of Sergio, Nella, and the others surrounding Cosimo. She had seen the shock sweep over poor Zuntura and had heard the words from those mouths, grasping everything and for the first time afflicted by this ability she had.

She flew off, and not finding Ciaccio at the bridge, searched for him afar and then further. Finally she found him.

She wanted to take him away, as far as possible, and thus chased away the sweet thought of dying in his lap. How wonderful it would have been!

She would have pressed her white back against her friend's skin and would have been received with open arms. Calmly, unhurriedly, then, she would have folded up her wings and her blue plumage would have disappeared from the world's view. Ciaccio would have caressed her gently as another blue, the sky, would have exploded in all of its magnificence in the eyes of both. That would have been the perfect time to go.

But she couldn't leave Ciaccio, and she didn't want to. She knew one thing: everything we lose or want to forget, the discarded words, the steps not taken, the choices not made—one day they will come up from the horizon and overtake the sun.

She gave Ciaccio another kiss and then rose up in flight.

Ciaccio followed her, and together they headed for that sun.

END

Luca Ragagnin

Luca Ragagnin was born in Turin, Italy in 1965. A prize-winning author, playwright, and poet, he was also a lyricist for multiple pop rock bands in the mid-1990s. Some of his works have been translated into multiple languages. He currently lives in Turin.

Mary Jean Lutz-Bujdos

After thirty-five years of teaching Italian and other related subjects at a variety of universities and venues, Mary Jean Lutz-Bujdos is an emerging literary translator. She divides her time between her home in Pennsylvania and a former elementary school turned home-studio near Parma, Italy.

Jamie Richards

Jamie Richards is the translator of over fifty works of fiction, non-fiction, and graphic narrative from the Italian. Her writing and translation can be found in periodicals such as *The Los Angeles Review of Books*, *Granta*, *Firmament*, *The Florence Review*, *Asymptote*, and *Words Without Borders*. She has been an NEA translation fellow and holds an MFA in Literary Translation from the University of Iowa, where she was recently translator-in-residence.

Milton Keynes UK
Ingram Content Group UK Ltd.
UKHW021855231024
450133UK00016B/991